Amulet

Roberto Bolaño was born in Santiago, Chile, in 1953. He spent much of his adult life in Mexico and Spain, where he died at the age of fifty. His novel *The Savage Detectives* was named one of the best books of 2007 by the *Washington Post* and the *New York Times Book Review*. His posthumous masterpiece, *2666*, won the National Book Critics Circle Award in 2008.

Amulet

Roberto Bolaño

Translated from the Spanish
by Chris Andrews

PICADOR

First published 2006 by New Directions Books, New York,
and simultaneously by Penguin Books Canada

First published in Great Britain 2009 by Picador

First published in paperback in Great Britain 2009 by Picador

This edition published 2010 by Picador
an imprint of Pan Macmillan, a division of Macmillan Publishers Limited
Pan Macmillan, 20 New Wharf Road, London N1 9RR
Basingstoke and Oxford
Associated companies throughout the world
www.panmacmillan.com

ISBN 978-0-330-51049-3

Copyright © The Heirs of Roberto Bolaño 1999
Translation copyright © Chris Andrews 2006

Originally published as *Amuleto* by Editorial Anagrama, Spain;
published by agreement with Agencia Literaria Carmen Balcells,
Editorial Anagrama, and the Heirs of Roberto Bolaño.

135798642

A CIP catalogue record for this book is available
from the British Library.

Printed by CPI Mackays, Chatham ME5 8TD

Visit **www.picador.com** to read more about all our books
and to buy them. You will also find features, author interviews and
news of any author events, and you can sign up for e-newsletters
so that you're always first to hear about our new releases.

For Mario Santiago Papasquiaro
(Mexico City, 1953-1998)

In our misery we wanted to scream for help,
but there was no one there to come to our aid.

—Petronius

O N E

This is going to be a horror story. A story of murder, detection and horror. But it won't appear to be, for the simple reason that I am the teller. Told by me, it won't seem like that. Although, in fact, it's the story of a terrible crime.

I am a friend to all Mexicans. I could say I am the mother of Mexican poetry, but I better not. I know all the poets and all the poets know me. So I could say it. I could say one mother of a zephyr is blowing down the centuries, but I better not. For example, I could say I knew Arturito Belano when he was a shy seventeen-year-old who wrote plays and poems and couldn't hold his liquor, but in a sense it would be superfluous and I was taught (they taught me with a lash and with a rod of iron) to spurn all superfluities and tell a straightforward story.

What I can say is my name.

My name is Auxilio Lacouture and I am Uruguayan—I come from Montevideo—although when I get nostalgic, when homesickness wells up and overwhelms me, I say I'm a *Charrúa*, which is more or less the same thing, though not exactly, and it confuses Mexicans and other Latin Americans too.

Anyway, the main thing is that one day I arrived in Mexico without really knowing why or how or when.

I came to Mexico City in 1967, or maybe it was 1965, or 1962. I've got no memory for dates anymore, or exactly where my wanderings took me; all I know is that I came to Mexico and never went back. Hold on, let me try to remember. Let me stretch time out like a plastic surgeon stretching the skin of a patient under anesthesia. Let me see. When I arrived in Mexico León Felipe was still alive—what a giant he was, a force of nature—and León Felipe died in 1968. When I arrived in

Mexico Pedro Garfías was still alive—such a great, such a melancholy man—and Don Pedro died in 1967, which means I must have arrived before 1967. So let's just assume I arrived in Mexico in 1965.

Yes, it must have been 1965 (although I could be mistaken, it certainly wouldn't be the first time) and day after day, hour after hour, I orbited around those two great Spaniards, those universal minds, moved by a poet's passion and the boundless devotion of an English nurse or of a little sister looking after her older brothers. Like me, they were wanderers, although for very different reasons; nobody drove me out of Montevideo; one day I simply decided to leave and go to Buenos Aires, and after a few months or maybe a year in Buenos Aires, I decided to keep traveling, because by then I already knew that Mexico was my destiny and I knew that León Felipe was living in Mexico, and although I wasn't sure whether Don Pedro Garfías was living here too, deep down I think I could sense it. Maybe it was madness that impelled me to travel. It could have been madness. I used to say it was culture. Of course culture sometimes is, or involves, a kind of madness. Maybe it was a lack of love that impelled me to travel. Or an overwhelming abundance of love. Maybe it was madness.

If nothing else, this much is clear: I arrived in Mexico in 1965 and turned up at the apartments of León Felipe and Pedro Garfías and said, Here I am, at your service. I guess they liked me: I'm not unlikeable; tiresome sometimes, but never unlikeable. The first thing I did was to find a broom and set about sweeping the floor of their apartments, and then I washed the windows, and, whenever I got the chance, I asked them for money and did their shopping. And they used to say to me, with that distinctive Spanish accent which they never lost, that prickly little music, as if they were circling the *z*s and the *s*s, which made the *s*s seem lonelier and more sensuous, Auxilio, they'd say, that's enough bustling around, Auxilio, leave those papers alone, woman, dust and literature have always gone together. And I would look at them and think, How right they are, dust and literature, from the beginning, and since at the time I was avid for detail, I conjured up wonderful and melancholy scenes, I imagined books sitting quietly on shelves and the dust of the world creeping into libraries, slowly, persistently, unstoppably, and then I came to understand that books are easy prey for dust (I understood this but refused to accept it), I saw whirlwinds, clouds of dust gathering over a plain somewhere deep in my memory, and the clouds advanced until they reached Mexico City, the clouds that had come from my own private plain, which belonged to everyone although many refused to admit it, and those clouds covered everything with dust, the books I had read and those I was planning to read, covered them irrevocably, there was nothing to be done: however heroic my efforts with broom and rag, the dust was never going to go away, since it was an integral part of the books, their way of living or of mimicking something like life.

That was what I saw. That was what I saw, seized by a tremor that only I could feel. Then I opened my eyes and the Mexican sky appeared. I'm in Mexico, I thought, with the tail end of that tremor still slithering through me. Here I am, I thought. And the memory of the dust vanished immediately. I saw the sky through a window. I saw the light of Mexico City shifting over the walls. I saw the Spanish poets and their shining books. And I said to them: Don Pedro, León (how odd, I called the older and more venerable of the two simply by his first name, while the younger one was somehow more intimidating, and I couldn't help calling him Don Pedro!), let me take care of this, you get on with your work, you keep writing, don't mind me, just pretend I'm the invisible woman. And they would laugh, or rather León Felipe would laugh, although to be honest it was hard to tell if he was laughing or clearing his throat or swearing, he was like a volcano, that man, while Don Pedro Garfías would look at me and then look away, and his gaze (that sad gaze of his) would settle on something, I don't know, a vase, or a shelf full of books (that melancholy gaze of his), and I would think: What's so special about that vase or the spines of those books he's gazing at, why are they filling him with such sadness? And sometimes, when he had left the room or stopped looking at me, I began to wonder and even went to look at the vase in question or the aforementioned books and came to the conclusion (a conclusion which, I hasten to add, I promptly rejected) that Hell or one of its secret doors was hidden there in those seemingly inoffensive objects.

Sometimes Don Pedro would catch me looking at his vase or the spines of his books and he'd ask, What are you looking at, Auxilio, and I'd say, Huh? What? and I'd pretend to be dopey or miles away, but sometimes I'd come back with a question that might have seemed out of place, but was relevant, actually, if you thought about it. I'd say to him, Don Pedro, How long have you had this vase? Did someone give it to you? Does it mean something special to you? And he'd just stare at me, at a loss for words. Or he'd say: It's only a vase. Or: No, it doesn't have any special meaning. That's when I should have asked him, So why are you looking at it as if it hid one of the doors to Hell? But I didn't. I'd just say: Aha, aha, which was a tic I'd picked up from someone, sometime during those first months, my first months in Mexico. But no matter how many *ahas* issued from my mouth, my brain went on working. And once, I can laugh about it now, once when I was alone in Pedrito Garfías's study, I started looking at the vase that had captured that sad gaze of his, and I thought: Maybe it's because he has no flowers, there are hardly ever any flowers here, and I approached the vase and examined it from various angles, and then (I was coming closer and closer, although in a roundabout way, tracing a more or less spiral path toward the object of my observation) I thought: I'm going to put my hand into the vase's dark mouth. That's what I thought. And I saw my hand move forward, away from my body, and rise and hover over the vase's dark mouth, approaching its enameled lip, at which point a little voice inside me said: Hey, Auxilio, what are you doing, you crazy woman, and that was what saved me, I think, because straight away my arm froze and my hand hung limp, like a dead ballerina's, a few inches from that Hell-mouth, and after that I don't know what happened to me, though I do know what could have happened and didn't.

You run risks. That's the plain truth. You run risks and, even in the most unlikely places, you are subject to destiny's whims.

That time with the vase, I started crying. Or rather, the tears welled up and took me by surprise and I had to sit in an armchair, the only armchair Don Pedro had in that room, otherwise I think I would have fainted. I know my vision blurred at one point, anyway, and my legs began to give. And once seated, I was seized by a violent shaking, as if I was about to have some kind of attack. The worst thing was that all I could think about was Pedrito Garfías coming in and seeing me in that awful state. Except that I hadn't stopped thinking about the vase; I averted my gaze, but I knew (I'm not completely stupid) that it was there, in the room, standing on a shelf beside a silver frog, a frog whose skin seemed to have absorbed all the madness of the Mexican moon. Then, still shaking, I got up and walked over to that vase again, with, I think, the sensible intention of picking it up and smashing it on the floor, on the green tiles of that floor, and this time the path I traced toward the object of my terror was not a spiral but a straight line, admittedly rather hesitant, but straight nevertheless. And when I was a few feet from the vase, I stopped again and said to myself: If it isn't Hell in there, it's nightmares, and all that is lost, all that causes pain and is better forgotten.

Then I thought: Does Pedrito Garfías know what's hidden in his vase? Do poets have any idea what lurks in the bottomless maws of their vases? And if they know, why don't they take it upon themselves to destroy them?

That day I couldn't think about anything else. I left earlier than usual and went for a walk in Chapultepec Park. A soothing, pretty place. But however much I walked and admired my surroundings, I couldn't stop thinking about the vase in Pedro Garfías's study and his books and that sad gaze of his that settled sometimes on quite inoffensive things and sometimes on things that were extremely dangerous. And so, while my gaze slid over the walls of Maximiliano and Carlota's palace, or the trees multiplied in the surface of Lake Chapultepec, in my mind's eye all I could see was a Spanish poet looking at a vase with what seemed to be an all-embracing sadness. And that infuriated me. Or rather, it did to begin with. I wondered why he didn't do anything about it. Why did the poet sit there looking at the vase instead of taking

ROBERTO BOLAÑO

two steps (he would have looked so elegant taking those two or three steps in his unbleached linen trousers), picking up the vase with both hands, and smashing it on the floor. But then my anger subsided and, thinking it over as the breeze of Chapultepec Park ("picturesque Chapultepec," to quote Manuel Gutiérrez Nájera) caressed the tip of my nose, I came to realize that, over the years, Pedrito Garfías had already smashed his fair share of vases and other mysterious objects, countless vases, on two continents! So who was I to find fault with him, even if only in my mind, for being so resigned to the one in his study.

Once I was in that frame of mind, I even started looking for reasons to justify the continuing presence of the vase, and sure enough various reasons occurred to me, but what's the point of listing them, what purpose could that serve? All I knew for sure was that the vase was there, although it could also have been sitting on the ledge of an open window in Montevideo or on my father's desk, in Doctor Lacouture's old house, my father the doctor, who died so long ago I've almost forgotten him, and even now the pillars of oblivion are collapsing onto that house and desk.

So all I know for sure is that I visited the apartments of León Felipe and Pedro Garfías and helped them in whatever way I could, dusting their books and sweeping the floors, for example, and when they protested, I'd say to them, Don't mind me, you get on with your writing and let me take care of the logistical support, and León Felipe would laugh, but not Don Pedro, Pedro Garfías, what a melancholy man, he didn't laugh, he looked at me with those eyes like a lake at sundown, like one of those lakes high in the mountains that nobody visits, those terribly sad and tranquil lakes, so tranquil they don't seem to belong to this world, and he would say, Don't bother, Auxilio, or Thank you, Auxilio, and that was all. What a divine man. What an honorable man. He would stand there, motionless, and thank me. That was all and that was enough for me. Because I'm not very demanding. It doesn't take long to work that out. León Felipe used to call me *Bonita*, he'd say, You're priceless, Auxilio, and try to help me out with a few pesos, but usually when he offered me money I'd kick up an almighty fuss. I'm doing this because I *want* to, León Felipe, I would say, out of sheer, irresistible admiration. And León Felipe would pause for a moment, pondering my choice of words, while I put the money he had given me on his desk and went on with my work. I used to sing. While I was working I used to sing and it didn't matter to me whether I was paid for my work or not (although it would be hypocritical to say that I wasn't glad to be paid). But with them it was different; I preferred to work for free. I would have paid out of my own pocket simply to be there, among their books and papers, coming and going as I pleased. Although in return I did accept the gifts they offered me. León Felipe used to give me little Mexican clay figurines; where they came from I don't know, because he didn't have many in his apartment. I think he bought them specially for me. Such sad little figurines. They were so pretty. Tiny and pretty. They didn't conceal the gates to Heaven or Hell, they were just figurines made by Indians in Oaxaca, who sold them to traders, who resold them at much higher prices at markets and street stalls in Mexico City. Don Pedro Garfías used to give me philosophy books. I can still remember one by José Gaos, which I tried to read but didn't like. José Gaos was another Spaniard and he died in Mexico too. Poor José Gaos, I should have made more of an effort. When did he die? I think it was in 1968, like León Felipe, no, in 1969, so he might even have died of sadness. Pedrito Garfías died in 1967, in Monterrey. León Felipe died in 1968. One after another I lost all the figurines that León Felipe had given me. Now they're probably sitting on shelves

in rooftop rooms or proper apartments in Colonia
Nápoles or Colonia Roma or Colonia Hipódromo-
Condesa. The ones that didn't get broken, that is.
The broken ones must have nourished the dust of
Mexico City. I also lost the books Pedro Garfías
gave me. First the philosophy books and then,
inevitably, the poetry as well.

From time to time I feel as though my books
and figurines were with me still. But how could
they be? Are they somehow floating around me or
over my head? Have the figurines and books that I
lost over the years dissolved into the air of Mexico
City? Have they become part of the ash that blows
through the city from north to south and from
east to west? Perhaps. The dark night of the soul
advances through the streets of Mexico City sweep-
ing all before it. And now it is rare to hear singing,
where once everything was a song. The dust cloud
reduces everything to dust. First the poets, then
love, then, when it seems to be sated and about to
disperse, the cloud returns to hang high over your
city or your mind, with a mysterious air that means
it has no intention of moving.

T W O

As I was telling you, I was faithful and regular in my visits to León Felipe and Pedro Garfías; I didn't expect them to read my poems or take an interest in my personal problems, I was just trying to be useful, but that didn't take up all my time.

I had my own life to lead. I had a life apart from basking in the glow of those luminaries of Hispanic letters. I had other needs. I worked at various jobs. I looked for work. I went looking and I despaired. Because the living is easy in Mexico City, as everyone knows or presumes or imagines, but only if you have some money or a scholarship or a family or at least some measly casual job, and I had nothing; the long voyage that had brought me to "the most transparent region of the air" had stripped me of many things, including the inclination to take on any old job. So what I did was hang around the university, specifically the Faculty of Philosophy and Literature, doing what you might call volunteer work: one day I'd help type out Professor García Liscano's lectures, the next day I'd be translating in the French department, where very few of the staff had really mastered the language of Molière, not that my French is perfect, but compared to theirs, it was excellent, or I'd latch onto a theater group, and spend eight hours straight, I'm not kidding, watching them rehearse over and over, or going to fetch sandwiches, experimenting with the spotlights, reciting the speeches of all the actors in a whisper that no one else could hear, but which made me happy all the same.

Sometimes, not often, I found paid work; a professor would pay me out of his salary to be a kind of personal assistant, or the department heads or the faculty would put me on a contract for two weeks, a month, or sometimes a month and a half, with vague, ambiguous and mostly nonexistent duties, or the secretaries—who were so nice, I made friends with them all; they confided in me, told me about their heartaches and their hopes— made sure their bosses kept finding me odd jobs so that I could earn a few pesos. That was during the day. At night I led what you might call a bohemian life with the poets of Mexico City, which I found deeply rewarding and convenient too, since money was scarce at the time and I didn't always have enough to pay for lodgings. But most of the time I did. I shouldn't exaggerate. I had enough money to get by and the poets educated me in Mexican literature by lending me books, their own books of poems for a start (you know what poets are like), then the essentials and the classics, so my expenses were minimal.

Sometimes I'd go for a whole week without spending a peso. I was happy. The Mexican poets were generous and I was happy. That was when I began to get to know them all and they got to know me. I became a fixture in their group. I spent my days at the faculty, busy as a bee or, to be more precise, a cicada, coming and going in and out of the little offices, keeping up with all the gossip, all the affairs and divorces, keeping up with all the tragedies. Like the tragedy of Professor Miguel López Azcárate, whose wife left him, and who couldn't bear the pain; I knew all about it, the secretaries told me. One day in a corridor I joined a group discussing some aspect of Ovid's poetry; the poet Bonifaz Nuño was there, I think, Monterroso too, perhaps, and two or three young poets. Professor López Azcárate must have been there, though he didn't say a word until the end (when it came to Latin poetry Bonifaz Nuño was the only recognized authority). And what in the name of heaven did we talk about? I can't remember exactly. All I remember is that it had to do with Ovid and that Bonifaz Nuño was holding forth interminably. He was probably making fun of some novice translator of the *Metamorphoses*. And Monterroso was smiling and nodding quietly. And the young poets (or maybe they were only students, poor things) were following suit. Me too. I craned my neck and peered at them fixedly. And from time to time, I threw in an exclamation, over the shoulders of the students, which was like adding a little silence to the silence. And then at some point in that scene, which must have really occurred, I can't have dreamed it, Professor López Azcárate opened his mouth. He opened his mouth as if gasping for air, as if that faculty corridor had been suddenly sucked into an unknown dimension, and said something about the *Art of Love*, by Ovid, something that took Bonifaz Nuño by surprise and seemed to intrigue Monterroso, but the young poets or students didn't understand it, me neither, and then López Azcárate turned red, as if he simply couldn't bear the suffocation any longer, and a few tears, just a few, four or six, rolled down his cheeks and hung from his mustache, a black mustache that was beginning to go white at the tips and in the middle, a look that always struck me as curious in the extreme, like a zebra or something, a black mustache that was, in any case, incongruous, crying out for a razor blade or a pair of scissors, and if you looked López Azcárate in the face for long enough it became blindingly obvious that this mustache was an anomaly (and a voluntary one), and that a man with such an anomaly on his face was bound to come to a bad end.

A week later López Azcárate hanged himself from a tree and the news ran through the university like a terrified, fleet-footed animal. And when I heard the news it left me shrunken and shivering, but also amazed, because although it was bad news, without a doubt, the worst, it was also, in a way, exhilarating, as if reality were whispering in your ear: I can still do great things; I can still take you by surprise, you silly girl, you and everyone else; I can still move heaven and earth for love.

At night, however, I opened out, I began to

grow again, I became a bat, I left the university and wandered around Mexico City like a wraith (I can't in all honesty say like a fairy, although I would like to) and drank and talked and attended literary gatherings (I knew where to find them all) and counseled the young poets who came to see me even back then, though not as much as they would later on, and I had a kind word for each of them. What am I saying: a word! I had a hundred or a thousand words for every one of them; to me they were all grandsons of López Velarde, great-grandsons of Salvador Díaz Mirón, those brave, troubled boys, those downhearted boys adrift in the nights of Mexico City, those brave boys who turned up with their sheets of foolscap folded in two and their dog-eared volumes and their scruffy notebooks and sat in the cafés that never close or in the most depressing bars in the world, where I was the only woman, except, occasionally, for the ghost of Lilian Serpas (but more about Lilian later), and they gave me their poems to read, their verses, their fuddled translations, and I took those sheets of foolscap and read them in silence, with my back to the table where they were raising their glasses desperately trying to be ingenious or ironic or cynical, poor angels, and I plunged into those words (I can't in all honesty say into that river of words, although I would like to, since it wasn't so much a river as an inchoate babble), letting them seep into my very marrow, I spent a moment alone with those words choked by the brilliance and sadness of youth, with those splinters of a shattered dime-store mirror, and I looked at myself or rather *for* myself in them, and there I was! Auxilio Lacouture, or fragments of Auxilio Lacouture: blue eyes, blond hair going gray, cut in a bob, long, thin face, lined forehead, and the fact of my selfhood sent a shiver down my spine, plunged me into a sea of doubts, made me anxious about the future, the days approaching at the pace of a cruise ship, although the vision also proved that I was living in and with my time, the time I had chosen, the time all around me, tremulous, changeable, teeming, happy.

And so I came to the year 1968. Or 1968 came to me. With the benefit of hindsight I could say I felt it coming. I could say I had a wild hunch and it didn't catch me unawares. I foresaw, intuited or suspected it; I sniffed it on the wind from the very first minute of January; I anticipated and envisaged it even as the first (and last) piñata of that innocently festive January was smashed open. I could even go so far as to say that I smelled its scent in the bars and parks in February and March of that year; I sensed its preternatural quiet in the bookshops and the food stalls, while I stood eating a pork taco in the Calle San Ildefonso, staring at the church of Saint Catherine of Siena and the Mexican dusk swirling deliriously, before the year 1968 was what it would become.

Ah, it makes me laugh to think about it now. It makes me want to cry! Am I crying? I saw it all and yet I didn't see a thing. Am I making any sense? I am the mother of all the poets, and I (or my destiny) refused to let the nightmare overcome me. Now the tears are running down my ravaged cheeks. I was at the university on the eighteenth of September when the army occupied the campus and went around arresting and killing indiscriminately. No. Not many people were killed at the university. That was in Tlatelolco. May that name live forever in our memory! But I was at the university when the army and the riot police came in and rounded everyone up. Unbelievable. I was in the bathroom, in the lavatory on one of the floors of the faculty building, the fourth maybe, I'm not exactly sure. And I was sitting in a stall, with my skirt hitched up, as the poem says, or the song, reading the exquisite poetry of Pedro Garfías, who had already been dead for a year (Don Pedro Garfías, such a melancholy man, so sad about Spain and the world in general). Who could have imagined that I would be reading in the bathroom just when the damned riot police came into the university? Now I believe, if you'll excuse a brief digression, that life is full of enigmas, minimal events that, at the slightest touch or glance, set off chains of consequences, which, viewed through the prism of time, invariably inspire astonishment or fear. The fact is that thanks to Pedro Garfías, thanks to the poems of Pedro Garfías and my inveterate habit of reading in the bathroom, I was the last to realize that the riot police were on campus and that the army had occupied the university, and so, while my eyes were scanning verses penned by that Spaniard who had died in exile, the soldiers and riot police were arresting and searching and beating up whoever they could lay their hands on, irrespective of sex or age, marital status or professional credentials acquired one way or another in the intricate, hierarchical world of the academy.

Let's just say I heard a noise.

A noise in my soul!

And let's say the noise grew steadily louder and soon I was alert to what was happening; I heard someone pull the chain in the next stall, I heard a door slamming, footsteps in a corridor, and a roar coming up from the gardens, from that carefully tended lawn that encompasses the faculty like a green sea lapping around an island ever propitious to the sharing of secrets and love. And then the bubble of Pedro Garfías's poetry went *pop* and I shut the book and stood up; I pulled the chain, opened the door, said something out loud, I said, Hey, is anyone there? But I knew full well that no one was going to answer. Do you know the feeling, as if you were in a horror movie, not the sort that has stupid women characters, but a film in which the women are intelligent and brave, or there is at least one brave, intelligent woman who suddenly finds herself alone, who suddenly walks into an empty building or an abandoned house and calls out (because she doesn't know the place is empty) to check if anyone is there; she raises her voice and asks the question, although her tone leaves no doubt as to the answer, but she asks anyway. Why? Well, basically because she was brought up, like me, to be polite in all circumstances. She stands there quietly or perhaps takes a few steps and asks if anyone is there and of course no one replies. I felt like that woman, although I don't know if I realized it at the time or if I'm only realizing it now, and, like her, I took a few steps as if I were walking on an enormous expanse of ice. Then I washed my hands, looked at myself in the mirror, saw a tall thin figure with a face that was already showing a few wrinkles, too many, a female Don Quixote as Pedro Garfías called me, and then I went out into the corridor, and there I realized right away that something was going on: the corridor was empty, nothing but faded shades of cream, and up the stairwell came a sound of shouting, a petrifying, history-making sound.

What did I do then? What anyone would have done: I went to a window and looked down and saw the soldiers, then I went to another window and saw tanks, and then to another, the one at the end of the corridor (I bounded down that corridor like a woman raised from the dead) and there I saw trucks, and the riot police and some plainclothes cops bundling the students and professors they'd arrested into the trucks, like something from a movie about the Second World War crossed with one about the Mexican Revolution starring María Felix and Pedro Armendáriz, a scene fading to black, but with little phosphorescent figures, like the ones some people see when they go crazy or have a sudden panic attack. I saw a group of secretaries, and I thought I could recognize some of my friends among them (in fact I thought I could recognize them all!), coming out in single file, tidying their clothes, with their handbags in their hands or over their shoulders, and then I saw a group of professors also coming out in an orderly fashion, or at least as orderly as the situation allowed, I saw people with books in their hands, people with folders and typed pages spilling onto the ground, bending down to pick them up, and I saw people being dragged out of the faculty building or coming out covering their noses with white handkerchiefs, which were rapidly darkening with blood. And then I said to myself: You stay here, Auxilio. Don't let them take you prisoner, my girl. Stay here, Auxilio, you don't have to be in that movie; if they want to make you play a role, they can damn well come and find you.

And then I went back to the bathroom, and this is the really strange part, not only did I go back to the bathroom, I went back to the stall, the very same stall I was in before, and I sat down on the toilet again, I mean, with my skirt hitched up again and my underpants down, although I felt no pressing physiological need (this is precisely the sort of situation that loosens the bowels, so they say, but that certainly wasn't the case with me), and the book of poems by Pedro Garfías open again on my lap, and although I didn't feel like reading I began to read, slowly at first, word by word and verse by verse, but then my reading started to speed up and soon it sped out of control, the verses flying past so quickly I could hardly take anything in, the words were sticking to one another, or something, in any case the poetry of Pedro Garfías could not withstand that free-fall reading (some poets and poems can withstand any kind of reading, but they are rare exceptions; most can't), and that's how I was occupied when I heard a sound in the corridor. A sound of boots? A sound of hobnailed boots? But, Hey, I said to myself, that would be too much of a coincidence, don't you think? The sound of hobnailed boots! But, Hey, I said to myself, all I need now is for it to be cold and a beret to drop on my head, and then I heard a voice saying something like, All clear, Sir, and five seconds later, someone, maybe the son of a bitch who had spoken before, opened the door of the bathroom and came in.

THREE

And I, poor creature that I was, heard something like the sound of the wind when it drops and rustles through paper flowers, I heard a flowering of air and water, and lifted my feet (quietly) like a Renoir ballerina, as if I were about to give birth (and in a sense, in effect, I was preparing to deliver something and to be delivered myself), with my underpants around my skinny ankles like a pair of handcuffs, hooked on my shoes (a pair of very comfortable yellow moccasins I had at the time). While I, a poor Uruguayan poet, but with a love of Mexico as deep as anyone's, waited for the soldier to search the cubicles one by one and prepared myself mentally and physically not to open the door, if it came to that, to defend the autonomy of the National Autonomous University of Mexico even in this last redoubt, a special kind of silence prevailed, a silence that figures neither in musical nor in philosophical dictionaries, as if time were coming apart and flying off in different directions simultaneously, a pure time, neither verbal nor composed of gestures and actions. And then I saw myself and I saw the soldier who was staring entranced at his image in the mirror, our two faces embedded in a black rhombus or sunk in a lake, and a shiver ran down my spine, alas, because I knew that for the moment the laws of mathematics were protecting me, I knew that the tyrannical laws of the cosmos, which are opposed to the laws of poetry, were protecting me and that the soldier would stare entranced at his image in the mirror and I, in the singularity of my stall, would hear and imagine him, entranced in turn, and that our singularities, from that moment on, would be joined like the two faces of a terrible, fatal coin.

To put it plainly: the soldier and I remained as still as statues in the women's bathroom on the fourth floor of the Faculty of Philosophy and Literature, and that was all. Then I heard his footsteps receding, I heard the door shutting, and my raised legs resumed their original position as if of their own initiative.

The birth was over.

I estimate that I must have spent about three hours sitting there.

I know that it was starting to get dark when I came out of the stall. My extremities had gone numb. There was a rock in my stomach and my chest hurt. There was gauze or a kind of veil in front of my eyes. There was a buzzing of blowflies or bees or wasps in my ears or in my mind. I felt ticklish and sleepy at the same time. But in fact I was more awake than ever. The situation was, admittedly, unfamiliar, but I knew what to do.

I knew where my duty lay.

I climbed up to the only window in the bathroom and peered out. I saw a lone soldier far off in the distance. I saw the silhouette or the shadow of a tank, although on reflection I suspected that it might have been the shadow of a tree. It was like the portico of portico of Latin or Greek literature. Ah, how I love Greek literature, from Sappho to George Seferis! I saw the wind sweeping through the university as if to savor the last of the daylight.

And I knew what I had to do. I knew. I knew that I had to resist. So I sat down on the tiles of the women's bathroom and, before the last rays of sunlight faded, read three more of Pedro Garfías's poems, then shut the book and shut my eyes and said: Auxilio Lacouture, citizen of Uruguay, Latin American, poet and traveler, resist.

That's all.

Then I began to think about my past as I am doing now. As I went back through the dates, the rhombus shattered in a space of speculative desperation, images rose from the bottom of the lake, no one could stop them emerging from that pitiful body of water, unlit by sun or moon, and time folded and unfolded itself like a dream. The year 1968 became the year 1964 and the year 1960 became the year 1956. But it also became the years 1970 and 1973 and the years 1975 and 1976. As if I had died and was viewing the years from an unaccustomed vantage point. I mean: I started thinking about my past as if I was thinking about my present, future, and past, all mixed together and dormant in the one tepid egg, the enormous egg of some inner bird (an archaeopteryx?) nestled on a bed of smoking rubble. For one thing I started thinking about the teeth I had lost, although at the time, in September 1968, I still had all my teeth, which is odd, to say the least, even on reflection. Nevertheless I thought about them, those four front teeth I lost one by one over the years because I didn't have the money or the inclination or the time to go to the dentist. And it was strange to be thinking about my teeth, because in a sense I didn't care that I had lost the four most important teeth in a woman's mouth, and yet in another sense their loss had left a deep wound in my being, a burning wound that was necessary and unnecessary, absurd. Even now, when I think about it, I still can't understand. Anyway, I lost my teeth in Mexico, where I had lost so many other things, and although from time to time friendly or at least well-meaning voices would say to me, Get some dentures, Auxilio, we'll take up a collection to buy you some, Auxilio, I always knew that the gap would go on gaping to the end like a wound, and I didn't pay them much attention, although I didn't refuse outright.

The loss gave rise to a new habit. From then on, whenever I talked or laughed, I covered my depleted mouth with the palm of my hand, a gesture that, as I soon discovered, was taken up and imitated in certain circles. I lost my teeth but not my discretion, my tact, my sense of propriety. The Empress Josephine, it is said, had enormous black cavities in her back teeth, but that did not diminish her charm by one iota. She covered her mouth with a handkerchief or a fan. In my lowlier station as a denizen of Mexico DF, that skyward and subterranean city, I placed the palm of my hand before my lips and laughed and spoke freely throughout the long Mexican nights. For those who made my acquaintance at the time, I must have seemed like a conspirator or some strange creature, half Shulamite, half albino bat. But that didn't matter to me. There's Auxilio, said the poets, and there I was, sitting at the table of a novelist with delirium tremens, or of a suicidal journalist, laughing and talking, whispering and gossiping, and no one could say: I have seen the wounded mouth of the woman from Uruguay, I have seen the bare gums of the only person who stayed in the university when it was occupied by the riot police in September 1968. They could say: Auxilio talks like a conspirator, bending close and covering her mouth. They could say: Auxilio looks you in the eyes when she speaks. They could say (with a laugh): How is it that Auxilio, who is constantly fiddling with a book or a glass of tequila, always manages to raise one hand to her mouth, in that spontaneous, natural-seeming way? What's the secret of her prodigious dexterity? Now, since I'm not planning to take that secret to the grave (where there's no point taking anything), I'll tell you, my friends: it's all in the nerves. The nerves that tense and relax as you approach the edges of companionship and love. The razor-sharp edges of companionship and love.

I lost my teeth on the altar of human sacrifice.

F O U R

But my teeth, which still hadn't fallen out, were not all that I thought about. For example, I thought about young Arturo Belano, who was sixteen or seventeen when I met him in 1970. I was the mother of the new Mexican poetry and he was just a kid who couldn't hold his liquor, but he was proud that Salvador Allende had been elected president of his faraway Chile.

I met him. I met him at a rowdy gathering of poets in a bar called the Encrucijada Veracruzana, a

ROBERTO BOLAÑO

squalid hole or dive where a motley bunch of
young and not-so-young hopefuls used to get
together now and then. He was the youngest hope-
ful of the lot. And the only one who had written a
novel at the age of seventeen. A novel that was later
lost or consumed by flames or perhaps it ended up
in one of the huge garbage dumps that surround
Mexico City; in any case I read it, with reservations
at first, but then with pleasure, not because it was
good, no, what I liked were the signs of determina-
tion on each page, the touching determination of
an adolescent: the novel was bad, but he was good.
So I made friends with him. It helped that we were
the only two South Americans among so many
Mexicans. I made friends with him, I went over
and talked to him, covering my mouth with my
hand, and he looked me in the eye, looked at the
back of my hand, and didn't ask why I was cover-
ing my mouth, but I think he guessed straight
away, unlike the others, I mean he guessed the
deeper reason, the ultimate dignity that obliged me
to cover my lips, and it didn't matter to him.

That night I made friends with him, in spite of
the difference in our ages, and all the other differ-
ences! I was the one who introduced him, some
weeks later, to the poetry of Ezra Pound and
William Carlos Williams and T. S. Eliot. I took

him home once, sick and drunk, holding him up as he clung to my bony shoulder, and I made friends with his mother and his father, and his sister, who was so nice, they were all so nice.

And the first thing I said to his mother was: I haven't slept with your son, Mrs. Belano. That's just how I am, I like to be frank and forthright with frank and forthright people (although this inveterate habit of mine has caused me no end of grief). I lifted my hands and smiled, then lowered them again and spoke, and she looked at me as if I had just stepped out of her son's notebooks, the notebooks of Arturito Belano, who by then was sleeping it off in his cavelike bedroom. And she said: Of course not, Auxilio, but there's no need to call me Mrs., we must be nearly the same age. And I raised an eyebrow and fixed her with the bluer of my eyes, the right one, thinking: She's right, kid, we must be more or less the same age. I might have been three years younger than her, or two, or one, but basically we belonged to the same generation; the only difference was that she had an apartment and a job and a monthly salary and I didn't; the only difference was that I went out with young people and Arturito's mother went out with people her own age; the only difference was that she had two teenage children and I had none, but that didn't matter either because by then I had children too, in my own way, hundreds of them.

So I became a friend of the family. A family of traveling Chileans who had emigrated to Mexico in 1968. My year. And sometimes I would say to Arturo's mother: You know, when you were getting ready to move, I was shut up in the women's bathroom on the fourth floor of the Faculty of Philosophy and Literature at the UNAM. I know, Auxilio. Funny, isn't it? Sure is. And we could go on like that for a fair while, at night, listening to music and talking and laughing.

I became a friend of the family. They invited me to stay at their apartment for long periods, a month, two weeks, or a month and a half, because at the time I had no money for a boarding house or a rooftop room and I had taken to wandering around, blown this way and that by the night winds that sweep the streets and avenues of Mexico City.

By day I busied myself at the university; by night I led a bohemian life, and slept, and gradually scattered my few belongings, leaving them in the houses and apartments of friends: my clothes, my books, my magazines, my photos. I, Remedios Varo, I, Leonora Carrington, I, Eunice Odio, I, Lilian Serpas (ah, poor Lilian Serpas, I still have to tell you about her). And my friends, of course, would eventually get tired of me and ask me to leave. And I would leave. I would crack a joke and leave. I would try to make light of it and leave. I would hang my head and leave. I would give them a kiss on the cheek and say thanks and leave. Some spiteful people say that I wouldn't go. They're lying. I would leave as soon as I was asked. Maybe, on one occasion, I shut myself in the bathroom and shed a few tears. Some gossipmongers say that I had a weakness for bathrooms. They couldn't be further from the truth. Bathrooms were a nightmare for me, although since September 1968, I had grown accustomed to nightmares. You can get used to anything. I like bathrooms. I like my friends' bathrooms. I like to take a shower and face the day with a clean body, who doesn't? I also like to shower before going to bed. Arturito's mother used to say to me: Use the clean towel I've put out for you, Auxilio, but I never used towels. I preferred to get dressed while my skin was still wet and let my body warmth evaporate the droplets of water. People used to find that funny. I found it funny too.

Although I could also have gone crazy.

But one thing stopped me from going crazy: I never lost my sense of humor. I could laugh at my skirts, my stovepipe trousers, my stripy tights, my white socks, my page-boy hair going whiter by the day, my eyes scanning the nights of Mexico City, my pink ears attuned to all the university gossip: the rises and falls, who got put down, who got passed over, who was sucking up to whom, the stars of the day, the inflated reputations, rickety beds that were taken apart and reassembled under the convulsive sky of

Mexico City, that sky I knew so well, that restless, unattainable sky, like an Aztec cooking pot, under which I came and went, happy just to be alive, with all the poets of Mexico City and Arturito Belano, who was seventeen years old, then eighteen, I could practically see him growing. They were all growing up under my watchful eye, not that it afforded them much protection. They were all growing up exposed to the storms of Mexico and the storms of Latin America, which are worse, if anything, because they are more divided and more desperate. And shimmering like moonlight in those storms, my gaze came to rest on the statues, the stunned figures, the groups of shadows, the silhouettes whose sole possession was a utopia of words, and fairly miserable words at that. Am I being unfair? No, it has to be admitted, their words were fairly miserable.

And I was there with them because I had nothing either, except my memories.

I could remember. I was still shut up in that women's bathroom in the faculty, lodged in the month of September 1968, and that was why I could be a dispassionate observer, although sometimes, thankfully, I did take part in the games of passion and love. Not all of my relationships were platonic. I slept with the poets. Not often, but from time to time I slept with one or the other. Despite appearances to the contrary, I was a woman and not a saint. And I did sleep with a number of them.

Usually it was a one-night stand: some drunken youth I led off to a bed or an armchair in an unoccupied room, while barbaric music I would rather not recall went on booming next door. When, occasionally, against the odds, it lasted longer than a night or a weekend, I would end up being more a psychotherapist than a lover. But I'm not complaining. Once my teeth went I was timid about kissing and being kissed, and how long can love last without kisses? Even so, I was hungry for sex. A hunger, that's the only word for it. You can't make love without that hunger. You need an opportunity too. But the hunger is the main thing.

Which reminds me of a story from those years that may be worth telling. I met a girl at the Faculty. It was during my theater phase. She was a charming girl. She had finished her philosophy degree. She was very cultured and elegant. I was sleeping in a seat at the faculty theater (a precarious institution to say the least) and dreaming of my childhood or of aliens. She sat down beside me. The theater, of course, was empty: on the stage a pitiful troupe was rehearsing a play by García Lorca. At some point I woke up, and she said to me: You're Auxilio Lacouture, aren't you, in such a friendly way that I liked her immediately. She had a slightly hoarse voice, and black, not very long hair, combed back. Then she said something funny or maybe I did, and we started laughing, quietly, so the director wouldn't hear us; he'd been a friend of mine in '68, but had since become a bad director and he knew it, which made him indiscriminately bitter. We left together and went out into the streets of Mexico City.

Her name was Elena and she bought me a coffee. She said she had a lot of things to tell me. She said she had been wanting to meet me for a long time. As we were leaving the faculty I realized she had a limp. Elena the philosopher. She had a Volkswagen and she took me to a café on Insurgentes Sur. I had never been there before. It was a lovely place, very expensive, but Elena had money and she really wanted to talk to me, although in the end I did all the talking. She listened and laughed and seemed happy, but she didn't say much. When we went our separate ways, I thought: What did she have to tell me, what did she want to talk about?

From then on we used to meet fairly regularly, in the theater or the corridors of the faculty, usually in the evening, as night was falling over the university, a time when some people don't know where to go or what to do with themselves. I would meet Elena and she would invite me for a drink or a meal in a restaurant on Insurgentes Sur. Once she invited me to her house in Coyoacán, a gorgeous house, tiny but gorgeous, very feminine and very intellectual, full of books about philosophy and theater, because Elena thought that philosophy and theater were closely related. She told me about that once, although I hardly understood a word she said. For me, theater is closer to poetry, but for her it's linked to philosophy—each to her own. And then all of a sudden she wasn't around. I don't know how much time went by. Months, maybe. Naturally I asked the faculty secretaries what had happened to Elena. Was she sick or traveling? Did they have any news of her? But no one could give me a convincing answer. One afternoon I decided to go to her house, but I got lost. I never get lost! Or at least not since September 1968. Before that, I did occasionally, not very often, lose my way in the labyrinth of Mexico City. But not after 1968. So there I was, searching for Elena's house, in vain, and I said to myself, There's something funny going on here, Auxilio, my girl, open your eyes and keep them peeled, or you might overlook the key to this story.

So I did. I opened my eyes and wandered around Coyoacán until eleven thirty at night, feeling more and more lost, more and more blind, as if poor Elena were dead or had never existed.

Some time went by. I quit being the theater's official hanger-on. I went back to the poets and my life took a new turn, there's not much point explaining why. All I know for sure is that I gave up helping my director friend from '68, not because I thought his directing was bad, although it was, but because I was bored, I needed a change of air, a change of scene, my spirit was hungry for a different kind of restlessness.

And one day, when I was least expecting it, I ran into Elena again. In the faculty cafeteria. There I was, conducting an impromptu survey of beauty in the student body, when suddenly I saw her, at a table off in a corner, and she seemed the same as ever at first, but as I approached, taking my time, I don't know why, stopping at each table on the way for a brief and rather awkward chat, I noticed that something had changed in her, although, for the moment, I couldn't identify what it was. When she saw me, and I'm certain of this, she greeted me with the same old warmth and friendliness. She was . . . I don't know how to put it. Maybe thinner, but no, she wasn't really any thinner. Maybe drawn, although she wasn't any more drawn than before. Maybe quieter, although after three minutes it was clear to me that she was no less talkative. Perhaps her eyelids were swollen. Perhaps her whole face was swollen, as if she were taking cortisone. But no. The evidence was there before my eyes: she was the same as ever.

We spent the evening and that whole night together. Starting in the cafeteria as it gradually emptied of students and professors, leaving only us in the end, and the cleaning lady, and the very nice, very sad middle-aged man behind the bar. Then we stood up to go (Isn't it dingy at this time of day, the cafeteria, she said; I didn't say what I thought at the time, but I can't see why I shouldn't now: to me, the cafeteria at that time of day was magnificent: shabby and majestic, indigent and absolutely free, shot through with the last rays of sunlight in the valley—that cafeteria was whispering to me, begging me to stay until the end and read a poem by Rimbaud, it was a cafeteria to weep for) and we got into her car and when we had already driven a fair way she said she was going to introduce me to an extraordinary guy, that's what she said, He's extraordinary, Auxilio, I want to you meet him and give me your opinion, although I realized straight away that my opinion wouldn't matter to her in the

ROBERTO BOLAÑO

least. She also said, After I introduce him to you,
you have to leave, I need to talk to him in private.
And I said, Of course, Elena, naturally. You intro-
duce him to me and then I'll go. A word to the wise
is enough. Anyway I have things to do tonight.
Like what, she asked. I have an appointment with
some poets on the Avenida Bucareli, I said. And
then we laughed like crazy and almost crashed the
car, but all the while I was thinking, and the more
I thought the clearer it became that Elena was not
well, though I couldn't give any specific, objective
reason for my assessment.

Meanwhile we had come to a place in the Zona
Rosa, a kind of bar, I've forgotten its name, but it
was in the Calle Varsovia and it specialized in wine
and cheese. It was the first time I'd been to a place
like that, such an expensive place, I mean, and I
must admit a ravenous hunger possessed me all of
a sudden, because although I'm as thin as a rake,
put food in front of me and I'm liable to fall upon
it like the Unrepentant Glutton of the Southern
Cone, or the Emily Dickinson of Bulimia, espe-
cially if it's an assortment of cheeses to beggar belief
and a variety of wines to set your head spinning. I
don't know what showed on my face, but Elena
took pity on me and said, Stay and eat with us,
although she also elbowed me discreetly as if to say:

Sure, stay and eat with us, but then make yourself scarce. I stayed to eat and drink with them and tried about fifteen different cheeses and drank a bottle of Rioja and met the extraordinary man, an Italian who was passing through Mexico and who, back in Italy, was friends, so he said, with Giorgio Strehler, and he liked me, at least thinking back now I realize he must have, because the first time I said I had to go, he said, Stay, Auxilio, what's the hurry, and the second time he said, Don't go, woman of wonderful conversation (his exact words), the night is young, and the third time I said I had to go, he said, That's enough, what are you fussing about, have Elena and I offended you or something? And then Elena elbowed me again, under the table, and in a perfectly calm and steady voice said, Stay, Auxilio, I'll give you a lift to wherever you need to go later on, and I looked at them and nodded, radiant with wine and cheese, not knowing what to do, whether to go or to stay, whether Elena's offer was genuine or really an invitation to do the opposite. And faced with that dilemma I decided that the best thing to do was to keep quiet and listen. Which is what I did.

The Italian's name was Paolo. That says it all, I think. He was born in a little village near Turin. He was at least six feet tall, had long brown hair and an enormous beard; Elena, or any other woman for that matter, could have disappeared into his embrace. Modern theater was his field but he hadn't come to Mexico to see theatrical performances. In fact the only thing he was doing in Mexico was waiting for a visa to Cuba, where he was planning to interview Fidel Castro. He had already been waiting for a long time. Once I asked him why they were taking so long. He told me that the Cubans wanted to check him out first. Only the right sort of people were granted an audience with Fidel Castro.

He had already been to Cuba twice, which, so he said, and Elena backed him up on this, was enough to make him suspicious in the eyes of the Mexican police, although I never noticed anyone who might have been a plainclothes cop watching him. They'd have to be doing a bad job for you to notice them, said Elena. Anyway Paolo's being watched by *secret* police agents. Which only proved my point, since it's common knowledge that secret police agents are the easiest to identify. A traffic cop, for example, take away his uniform and he could pass for a factory worker, some even look like union leaders, but a secret policeman will always look like a secret policeman.

We were friends from that night on. On

Saturdays and Sundays the three of us would go see the free plays at the Casa del Lago. Paolo liked to watch the amateur groups that used the open-air theater. Elena sat between us, leaned her head on Paolo's arm and soon fell asleep. She didn't like the amateur actors. I sat on Elena's right, and to tell the truth I didn't pay much attention to what was happening on stage, since I was always keeping an eye out to see if I could spot a secret police agent. And I did actually spot not one but several. When I told Elena, she burst out laughing. You couldn't have, Auxilio, she said, but I knew I wasn't mistaken. Then I realized what was going on. On Saturdays and Sundays the Casa del Lago was literally swarming with spooks, but they weren't all on Paolo's trail; most of them were there to watch other people. We knew some of the people under observation from the university or the world of independent theater and we used to say hello to them. Others were strangers to us, and we could only feel for them, imagining the paths they would trace with their pursuers in tow.

It didn't take me long to realize that Elena was very much in love with Paolo. What will you do when he finally goes to Cuba? I asked her one day. I don't know, she said, looking like a lonely little Mexican girl, and in that face I thought I saw a gleam or a pang that I had seen before, and I knew it wasn't a sign of good things to come. Nothing good ever comes of love. What comes of love is always something better. But better can sometimes mean worse, if you're a woman, if you live on this continent, hit upon unhappily by the Spaniards, inopportunely populated by Asians gone astray.

That's what I thought, shut up in the women's bathroom on the fourth floor of the faculty of Philosophy and Literature in September 1968. I thought about those Asians crossing the Bering Strait, I thought about the solitude of America, I thought about how strange it is to emigrate eastward rather than westward. I may be silly and I'm certainly no expert on the matter, but in these troubled times no one will deny that to migrate eastward is like migrating into the depths of the night. That's what I thought, sitting on the floor, with my back against the wall, gazing absently at the spots on the ceiling. Eastward. To where night comes from. But then I thought: It's also where the sun comes from. It all depends on when the pilgrims set out on their march. And then I struck my forehead (or tapped it, because I didn't have much strength after so many days without food) and I saw Elena walking down an empty street in Colonia Roma, I saw Elena walking eastward, toward the depths of the night, on her own, well dressed, limping; I saw her and I called out, Elena! But no sound at all came out of my mouth.

And Elena turned to me and said she didn't know what she was going to do. Maybe go to Italy. Maybe wait until he comes back to Mexico. I don't know, she said to me with a smile, but I knew that she knew very well what she was going to do and that she was already resigned to it. As for the Italian, he was happy to let her love him and show him around Mexico City. I can't remember all the places we went together: la Villa, Coyoacán, Tlatelolco (that time I didn't go, it was just him and Elena), the slopes of Popocatépetl, Teotihuacán, and everywhere we went the Italian was happy and Elena was happy too, and so was I, because I've always enjoyed sightseeing and the company of happy people.

One day, at the Casa del Lago, we even ran into Arturito Belano. I introduced him to Elena and Paolo. I told them he was an eighteen-year-old Chilean poet. I explained that he wrote plays as well as poems. Paolo said, How interesting. Elena didn't say anything because, by this stage, she was only interested in her relationship with Paolo. We went to have coffee at a place called El Principio de Mexico in the Calle de Tokio (it shut down a while back). I don't know why I remember that afternoon. That afternoon of 1971 or 1972. And the strangest thing is that I remember it prospectively, from 1968. From my watchtower, my bloody subway carriage, from my gigantic rainy day. From the women's bathroom on the fourth floor of the Faculty of Philosophy and Literature, the timeship from which I can observe the entire life and times of Auxilio Lacouture, such as they are.

And I remember that Arturito and the Italian talked about theater, Latin American theater, and Elena ordered a cappuccino and was rather quiet, and I started looking at the walls and the floor of El Principio de Mexico, and immediately noticed something odd—I always pick up on things like this—a sort of noise, wind or breath, blowing up through the foundations of the café at irregular intervals. And so the minutes went by, with Arturito and Paolo talking about theater, Elena sitting quietly, and me turning my head from time to time, attentive to the receding sounds of what, by then, was undermining not only the Principio de Mexico but the whole city, as if I were being warned a few years in advance or a few centuries too late about the fate of Latin American theater, the double nature of silence, and the collective catastrophe of which improbable sounds are often harbingers.

Improbable sounds and clouds. And then Paolo
stopped talking with Arturito and said that the visa
for Cuba had arrived that morning. And that was
it. The noises stopped. The pensive silence was bro-
ken. We forgot about Latin American theater, even
Arturito, who wasn't generally quick to let a subject
go, although the theater he preferred was not Latin
American at all but that of Beckett and Jean Genet.
And we started talking about Cuba and the inter-
view that Paolo was going to have with Fidel
Castro, and that was that. We said goodbye on
Reforma. Arturo was the first to leave. Then Elena
and her Italian went off. Which left me standing
there, drinking in the breeze on the avenue as I
watched them walk away. Elena's limp was more
pronounced than usual. I thought about Elena. I
breathed. I trembled. I watched her limp away with
the Italian at her side. And suddenly I could see
only her. The Italian began to disappear, becoming
transparent; all the people walking along Reforma
became transparent. All my aching eyes could make
out was Elena, with her overcoat and her shoes.
And then I thought: Resist, Elena. And then I
thought: Catch up with her and give her a hug. But
she was going off to live her last nights of love and
I couldn't disturb her.

After that I went for a long time without news

of Elena. No one knew anything. One of her friends said to me: Missing in action. Another said: Apparently she went to Puebla, to her parents' place. But I knew that Elena was in Mexico City. One day I went looking for her house and got lost again. Another day, at the university, I got hold of her address and took a taxi there, but no one came to the door. I went back to the poets, I went back to being a night owl and forgot about Elena. Sometimes I dreamed of her and saw her limping through the boundless campus of the UNAM. Sometimes I peered out of my window in the women's bathroom on the fourth floor and saw her approaching the faculty building amid a whirl of transparent forms. Sometimes I fell asleep on the tiled floor and heard her steps coming up the stairs, as if she were coming to rescue me, coming to say sorry for having taken so long. And I opened my mouth, half dead or half asleep, and said, *Chido*, Elena, quite uncharacteristically using that awful Mexican slang word for *great*. Chido, chido, chido. How awful. There's something masochistic about Mexican slang. Or sadomasochistic, sometimes.

That's the way love is, my friends; I speak as the mother of all the poets. That's the way love is, and slang, and the streets, and sonnets. And the sky at five in morning. But friendship is something different. If you have friends you're never alone.

I was friends with León Felipe and Don Pedro Garfías, but also with the youngest poets, the kids who lived in a lonely world of love and slang.

Arturito Belano was one of them.

I met him, I was his friend, and he was my favorite young poet, although he wasn't Mexican, and the expressions "young poets" and "new generation" were generally used to refer to the young Mexicans who were trying to take over from Pacheco or the conspicuous Greek of Guanajuato or the chubby little guy who was working in the Ministry of the Interior while waiting for the Mexican government to appoint him ambassador or consul somewhere, or the Peasant Poets, those four, or three, or five (I forget) horsemen of the Nerudian apocalypse, but Arturo Belano, in spite of being the youngest of them all, for a time at least, wasn't Mexican and therefore didn't fall into the category of "young poets" or "new generation," terms that designated a formless but living mass intent on pulling the rug out from under their elders or undermining the fertile fields on which they were grazing like statues: Pacheco and the Greek of Guanajuato or Aguascalientes or Irapuato, and the chubby little guy who, with the passage of time, had become a greasy, fat, obsequious man (as poets are prone to do), and the Peasant Poets, who were more and more comfortably ensconced in the administrative and literary bureaucracy (but what am I saying: they were lodged there, bolted down, deeply rooted from the very start). And what the young poets or the new generation were trying to do was to make the ground shift, to topple and in due course destroy those statues, except for Pacheco, the only one who seemed to be a real writer, not a public servant. But deep down they were against Pacheco too. Deep down they couldn't allow themselves to make any exceptions. So when I said to them, But José Emilio is charming, he's so kind, so interesting, and he's a real gentleman too, the young poets of Mexico (including Arturito, although he wasn't really one of them) looked at me as if to say, What's she going on about, this crazy woman, this specter escaped from that infernal women's bathroom on the fourth floor of the Faculty of Philosophy and Literature. Now most people, faced with that kind of stare, would quail, but not me, I was their mother, after all, and backing down was something I simply didn't do.

Once I told them a story I had heard José Emilio tell: if Rubén Darío hadn't died so young, before reaching the age of fifty, Huidobro would certainly have got to know him, much as Ezra Pound got to know W. B. Yeats. Imagine it: Huidobro working as Darío's secretary. But the young poets were too young to be able to grasp how important the encounter between the old Yeats and the young Pound had been for poetry in English (and, in fact, for poetry all around the world), so they didn't realize how important the

ROBERTO BOLAÑO

hypothetical encounter and the potential friend-
ship between Darío and Huidobro might have
been; they had no sense of the range of missed
opportunities for poetry in our language. Because
Darío, I dare say, would have taught Huidobro a
great deal, but Huidobro would also have taught
Darío a thing or two. That's how the relationship
between master and disciple works: it is not only
the disciple who learns. And since we're speculat-
ing, I believe, and so did Pacheco (with an innocent
enthusiasm that is one of his great qualities), that,
of the two, Darío would have learned more; he
would have been able to bring Hispanic mod-
ernism to a close and begin something new, not the
avant-garde as such, but an island, say, between
modernism and the avant-garde, what we might
now call the non-existent island, an island of words
that never were, and could only have come into
being (granted that this were even possible) after
the imaginary encounter between Darío and
Huidobro; and Huidobro himself, after his fruitful
encounter with Darío, would have been able to
found an even more vigorous avant-garde, what we
might name the non-existent avant-garde, which,
had it existed, would have transformed us and
changed our lives. That's what I said to the young
poets of Mexico (and Arturito Belano) when they

were bad-mouthing José Emilio, but they didn't listen to me, or only to the anecdotes about the travels of Darío and Huidobro, their illnesses, their hospitals, but also the other kind of health they had, not condemned to fail prematurely, as so many things in Latin America fail.

And then I kept quiet while they went on bad-mouthing the poets of Mexico, the ones they were going to blow out of the water, and I thought about the dead poets, like Darío and Huidobro, and about all the encounters that never occurred. The truth is that our history is full of encounters that never occurred. We didn't have our Pound or our Yeats; we had Huidobro and Darío instead. We had what we had.

And, at the risk of overstretching every imagination but my own, which is supreme in its elasticity, I will say that some nights my friends even seemed, for a second, to be the incarnations of those who had never come into existence: the Latin American poets who died in childhood, at the age of five or ten, or just a few months after they were born. This exercise in vision was difficult, and futile too, or so it seemed, but, by the purplish light of certain nights, I could see through the features of my friends to the little faces of the babies who never grew up. I saw the little angels they bury in

ROBERTO BOLAÑO

shoeboxes in Latin America, or in little wooden coffins painted white. And sometimes I said to myself: These kids are our hope. But other times I thought: Some hope, a bunch of drunk kids—all they can do is run down José Emilio—a band of young drunkards versed in the art of hospitality but not in the art of verse.

And then the young poets of Mexico began to recite poetry in their deep but irreparably juvenile voices, and the lines they recited went blowing in the wind through the streets of Mexico City, and I began to cry, and they said, Auxilio's drunk (the fools, it takes a lot more than that to get me drunk), or, She's crying because what's-his-name left her, and I let them say whatever they liked. Or I argued with them. Or insulted them. Or got up from my chair and left without paying—I never paid, or hardly ever. I was the one who could see into the past and those who can see into the past never pay. But I could also see into the future and vision of that kind comes at a high price: life, sometimes, or sanity. So I figure I was paying, night after forgotten night, though nobody realized it; I was paying for everyone's round, the kids who would be poets and those who never would.

I left without paying, or so it seemed. I didn't have to pay because I could see the whirlwind of the past that swept like a breath of hot air through the streets of Mexico City, smashing the windows of the buildings. But I could also see the future from my obliterated cave in the fourth-floor women's bathroom, and for that I was paying with my life. So when I left I was paying after all, though nobody knew. I was paying for myself and for the young poets of Mexico and for the anonymous alcoholics of whatever bar we happened to be in that night. Off I went staggering through the streets of Mexico City, pursuing my elusive shadow, alone and tearful, feeling like the last Uruguayan on the planet, which I wasn't, of course, how egotistical, and although I was picking my way through craters illuminated by hundreds of moons, they were not the craters of planet Earth but those of Mexico, a distinction that might appear to be, but is not, quite devoid of sense.

And one night I had the feeling that someone was following me. I don't know where we had been. Maybe in a bar on the outskirts of La Villa, maybe at some dive in Colonia Guerrero. I can't remember. I only know that I kept on walking, making my way through the rubble, without paying much attention to the footsteps that were following in my footsteps, until suddenly the nocturnal sun went out, I stopped crying, came back to reality with a

ROBERTO BOLAÑO

shudder and understood that the person following
me, whoever it was, desired my death. Or my life.
Or the tears I had shed on that hateful reality, as
harsh as our often intractable tongue. And then I
stopped and waited, and the steps that were echo-
ing my steps stopped and waited too, and I looked
around in the street for someone I knew, or a
stranger I could run to, crying for help, who could
take my arm and walk me to the nearest subway
station or stay with me until I hailed a cab, but I
couldn't see anyone. Or maybe I could. I saw some-
thing. I shut my eyes, then opened them, and I saw
the white tiled walls of the women's bathroom
on the fourth floor. Then I shut my eyes again and
heard the wind sweeping through the campus
around the Faculty of Philosophy and Literature
with a diligence worthy of a higher enterprise.
And I thought: History is like a horror story. And
when I opened my eyes a shadow peeled away from
a wall, moved onto the sidewalk about ten yards
ahead, and began to come toward me, and I put my
hand into my handbag, I mean my satchel from
Oaxaca, and felt for my knife, which I always car-
ried with me, as a precaution against urban emer-
gencies, but the burning skin of my fingertips
could feel only papers and books and magazines
and even clean underwear (washed by hand, with-

out soap, with water and sheer willpower, in one of the sinks of that dreamlike, omnipresent fourth-floor bathroom), but not the knife, ah, my friends, now there's another recurring and terribly Latin American nightmare: being unable to find your weapon; you know where you put it, but it's not there.

That's just our luck.

And it could have been mine. But when the shadow intent on my death, or at least on inflicting suffering and humiliation, approached the doorway where I had hidden, other shadows appeared in that street, which could have become the epitome of all the terrifying streets I had ever walked down, and called out to me: Auxilio, Auxilio, Socorro, Amparo, Caridad, Remedios Lacouture, Where have you gone? And I recognized the voice of the sad and clever Julián Gómez, while the other, brighter-sounding voice belonged to Arturito Belano, ready for a fight, as always. And then the shadow that was bent on my torment stopped, looked back and walked on, went past me: an ordinary-looking Mexican guy fresh out of the under-world, and with him passed a breath of warm and slightly humid air that conjured up unstable geometries, solitudes, schizophrenia, and butchery, and the absolute son of a bitch didn't even glance at me.

After that we went downtown, the three of us, and Julián Gómez and Arturito Belano continued their conversation about poetry, and two or three more poets joined us at the Encrucidada Veracruzana, or maybe they were just journalists or future college professors, and they all went on talking about poetry, new poetry, but I said nothing, I was listening to my heartbeat, still shaken by the encounter with that shadow, although I hadn't said a word about it, so I didn't notice when the discussion turned into an argument or when the shouting and the insults began. They chucked us out of the bar. We walked away through the empty streets of Mexico City at five in the morning and the group diminished as people peeled off, one by one, each heading for home, and at the time I had a place of my own to go to, a rooftop room in Colonia Roma Norte, in the Calle Tabasco, and since Arturito Belano lived in Colonia Juárez, on Versalles, we walked together, although, had he been navigating like a Cub Scout, he really should have turned off to the west, toward the Glorieta de Insurgentes or the Zona Rosa, since he lived right on the corner of Versalles and Berlin, while I had to keep going south. But Arturito Belano decided to go a bit out of his way and keep me company.

To tell the truth, at that hour of the night, nei-

ther of us was very talkative, and although now
and then we commented on the quarrel at the
Encrucijada Veracruzana, mostly we just walked
and breathed the air of Mexico City, which seemed
to have been purified by the dawn, until Arturito
said, in his most nonchalant tone of voice, that he
had been worried about me in that dive in La Villa
(so it was La Villa), and when I asked him why, he
said because he too (the angel) had seen the shadow
that was following my shadow. I looked at him
calm as you please, raised my hand to my mouth,
and said, It was the shadow of death, and although
he laughed incredulously, I wasn't offended at all. It
was as if he were saying, That was some bad trip
back there, Auxilio. I raised my hand to my mouth
again and stopped walking and said, If it hadn't
been for you and Julián, I'd be dead now. Arturito
listened, then walked on. And I caught up with
him and we walked side by side. And so, stopping
and talking, or walking on in silence, before we
knew it, we came to the doorway of the building
where I lived. And that was that.

Later, in 1973, when he decided to go back to
his country and take part in the revolution, I was
the only one, apart from his family, who went to
see him off at the bus station (because Arturito
Belano traveled overland). It was a long trip, long

and hazardous, an initiation, a Latin American
grand tour on a shoestring, wandering the length of
our absurd continent, which we keep misunder-
standing or simply not understanding at all. And
when Arturito waved goodbye from the window of
the bus, his mother cried, and so did I, inexplica-
bly, my eyes filled with tears, as if that boy were my
son too, and I was afraid I would never see him
again.

That night I slept at Arturo's place, mostly to
keep his mother company, and I remember we
stayed up late talking about women's things, not
exactly my usual topics of conversation. We talked
about children growing up and going out to play in
the big, wide world; we talked about the lives they
lead when they leave their parents and set off into
the big, wide world in search of the unknown.
Then we talked about the big, wide world itself. A
world that was not, in fact, so big or wide for us.
And then Arturo's mother read the tarot cards for
me and said that my life was about to change, and
I said, That's good, you know, a change is just
what I need right now. After that I made coffee, I
don't know what time it was, but it was very late,
and both of us must have been tired, although we
didn't let it show, and coming back into the living
room I found Arturo's mother laying out the cards

on a tiny table they had in the living room, and I stopped and watched her in silence: there she was, sitting on the sofa with a look of concentration on her face (although behind the concentration a degree of anxiety was also perceptible), her small hands turning the cards as if they had been extracted from her body. I realized straight away that she was reading her own future, and what she saw in the cards was terrible, but that didn't matter. What mattered was something a little harder to grasp. What mattered was that as she waited for me, alone, she was not afraid.

That night I would have liked to be more intelligent than I am. I would have liked to have been able to comfort her. But all I could do was bring her coffee and tell her not to worry, everything would turn out fine.

The next morning I left, although I had nowhere to go at the time, except the Faculty and the same old bars, cafés, and restaurants, but I went anyway. I don't like to overstay my welcome.

When Arturo returned to Mexico in January 1974, he was different. Allende had been overthrown, and Arturito had done his duty, so his sister told me; he'd obeyed the voice of his conscience, he'd been a brave Latin American boy, and so in theory there was nothing for him to feel guilty about.

When Arturo returned to Mexico, he was a stranger to all his old friends, except for me. That was because, the whole time he was gone, I stayed in touch with his family. I was a regular visitor at their apartment. But not a nuisance. I didn't stay the night; I would just pop in, chat for a while with his mother or his sister (not his father, who didn't like me), and then I'd leave and not come back for a month or so. That's how I found out about his adventures in Guatemala and El Salvador (where he stayed for quite a while with a friend called Manuel Sorto, who'd also been a friend of mine), and in Nicaragua, Costa Rica, and Panama. In Panama he got into a fight with a big black guy at a border crossing. We had such a good laugh over that letter, his sister and me! The guy was six foot three and must have weighed sixteen stone, according to Arturo, who was five foot nine, and eleven and half stone at the most. Then he got on a boat in Cristóbal and the boat took him down the Pacific coast to Colombia, Ecuador, Peru, and finally Chile.

I ran into his sister and his mother at the first demonstration in Mexico after the coup. They hadn't heard from him and we all feared the worst. I remember that demonstration; it might even have been the first protest against the overthrow of Allende in the whole of Latin America. I saw a few familiar faces from 1968, a few diehards from the faculty, but most of all I saw generous young Mexicans. I also saw something else: I saw a mirror and, peering into it, I could see an enormous, unin-habited valley, and the vision of that valley brought tears to my eyes, partly because, at the time, the most trifling matters were enough to make me burst into tears. The valley I had seen, however, was no trifling matter. I don't know if it was the vale of joy or the vale of tears. But I saw it and then I saw myself shut up in the women's bathroom, and I remembered that there I had dreamed of the very same valley, and waking from that dream or night-mare I had begun to cry or maybe it was the other way around, maybe the tears had woken me. And the dream of September 1968 reappeared in that September of 1973, which must mean something, surely, it can't have been purely coincidental; no one can elude the combinations or permutations or dispositions of chance. Perhaps Arturito is already dead, I thought, perhaps that lonely valley is an emblem of death, because death is the staff of Latin America and Latin America cannot walk without its staff. But then Arturo's mother took me by the arm (I was in a kind of daze) and we marched on together shouting *El pueblo unido jamás será venci-do*, ah, it makes my cry to think of it now.

Two weeks later I talked with his sister on the phone and she told me that Arturo was alive. I sighed. What a relief. But I had to keep going. I was the itinerant mother. The wanderer. Life drew me into other stories.

One night, at a party in Colonia Anzures, propped on my elbows in a sea of tequila, watching a group of friends trying to break open a piñata in the garden, it occurred to me that it was an ideal time to call Arturo's place. His sister answered the phone. Merry Christmas, I said. Merry Christmas, she replied sleepily. Then she asked where I was. With some friends. What's with Arturo? He's coming back to Mexico next month. When exactly? We don't know. I'd like to go to the airport, I said. Then for a while we said nothing and listened to the party noises coming from the patio. Are you feeling OK, his sister asked. I'm feeling strange. Well that's normal for you. Not all that normal; most of the time I feel perfectly well. Arturo's sister was quiet for a bit, then she said that actually she was feeling pretty strange herself. Why's that? I asked. It was a purely rhetorical question. To tell the truth, both of us had plenty of reasons to be feeling strange. I can't remember what she said in reply. We wished each other a merry Christmas again and hung up.

A few days later, in January 1974, Arturito arrived from Chile and he was different.

What I mean is that although he was the same

Arturo, deep down something had changed or grown, or changed and grown at the same time. What I mean is that people, his friends, began to see him differently, although he was the same as ever. What I mean is that everyone was somehow expecting him to open his mouth and give us the latest news from the Horror Zone, but he said nothing, as if what other people expected had become incomprehensible to him or he simply didn't give a shit.

His best friends were no longer the young poets of Mexico, who were all older than him in any case; he started hanging out with adolescent poets, all younger than he was: sixteen-, seventeen-, eighteen-year-old kids, who seemed to have graduated from the great orphanage of Mexico City's subway rather than from the Faculty of Philosophy and Literature. Sometimes I'd see them peering through the windows of the cafés and bars on Bucareli, and the mere sight made me shudder, as if they weren't creatures of flesh and blood but a generation sprung from the open wound of Tlatelolco, like ants or cicadas or pus, although they couldn't have been there or taken part in the demonstrations of '68; these were kids who, in September '68, when I was shut up in the bathroom, were still in junior high school. And they were Arturito's new friends.

I wasn't immune to their beauty. I'm not immune to any kind of beauty. But, shuddering at the sight of them, I realized that they didn't speak the same language as me or the young poets. What those poor orphaned strays were saying was incomprehensible to José Agustín, the novelist in fashion at the time, and to the young poets who wanted to overthrow José Emilio Pacheco, and to José Emilio himself, who was dreaming of the impossible encounter between Darío and Huidobro. No one could understand those voices, which were saying: We're not from this part of Mexico City, we come from the subway, the underworld, the sewers, we live in the darkest, dirtiest places, where the toughest of the young poets would be reduced to retching.

All things considered, it wasn't really surprising that Arturo started hanging out with them and gradually distanced himself from his old friends. They were the children of the sewers and Arturo had always been a child of the sewers.

He still kept up with one of his old friends, however. Ernesto San Epifanio. I met Arturo first, then I met Ernesto San Epifanio, one radiant night in 1971. Arturo had been the youngest of the group. Then Ernesto came along, and he was a year or a few months younger, so Arturito had to yield his ambivalent place of honor. But there was no tension or jealousy between them, and when Arturo returned from Chile, in January 1974, Ernesto San Epifanio went on being his friend.

What happened between them was very odd. And I'm the only one who can tell the story. At the time, Ernesto San Epifanio seemed to have some kind of illness. He was hardly eating and had become very thin. At night, throughout those Mexico City nights canopied with sheet upon linen sheet, he drank but ate nothing, hardly talked to anyone, and when we went out into the street, he looked around as if he were afraid of something. When his friends asked what was going on, he remained silent or replied with some quote from his beloved Oscar Wilde, but even his characteristic wit had grown sluggish, and those quips, delivered so despondently, provoked only puzzlement and pity. One night I passed on some news about Arturo (which I'd heard from his mother and his sister) and Ernesto listened to me as if he was thinking that going to live in Pinochet's Chile might not actually be such a bad idea.

For the first few days after returning, Arturo stayed at home, hardly setting foot outside, and, for everyone but me, it was as if he still hadn't come back from Chile. But I went to his apartment and talked to him and found out that he'd been imprisoned, for eight days, and although he hadn't been tortured, he'd acquitted himself bravely. And I told his friends. I said, Arturito's back, and I painted his return with colors borrowed from the palette of epic poetry. And when, one night, Arturito finally appeared in the Café Quito on the Avenida Bucareli, his old friends, the young poets, saw him in a different light. Why? Well, because for them, Arturito now belonged to the category of those who have seen death at close range, and the subcategory of hard men, and, that, in the eyes of those desperate Latin American kids, was a qualification that commanded respect, a veritable compendium of medals.

It also has to be said that, deep down, they remained somewhat skeptical. I mean I was the source of the legend; they heard it from my mouth, from my lips hidden by the back of my hand, so although everything I had said about him while he was shut up in his apartment was essentially true, the story wasn't altogether credible, simply because of its source; that is, me. That's how it is on this continent. I was the mother and they believed me, but they didn't believe *every* word I said. Except for Ernesto San Epifanio. During the days leading up to Arturo's public reappearance, Ernesto made me

tell and retell the story of our friend's adventures
at the ends of the earth, and with each repetition,
he became more enthusiastic. What I mean is that
as I talked and invented adventures, Ernesto San
Epifanio's lethargy gradually fell away, and his
melancholy too, or at least his lethargy and his
melancholy stirred, shook themselves and began to
breathe again. So when Arturo reappeared and
everyone wanted to be with him, Ernesto San
Epifanio was present along with the others, and
took part, albeit in a self-effacing way, in the wel-
come that Arturo's old friends organized for him,
which consisted, if I remember rightly, of standing
him a beer and a serving of *chilaquiles* at the Café
Quito, a modest repast by any standard, but well
matched to the economic resources at the group's
disposal. And when they all went home, Ernesto
San Epifanio remained, leaning against the bar of
the Encrucijada Veracruzana, since by then we had
moved on from the Quito, while Arturo sat alone
at a table, accompanied only by his ghosts, staring at
his last tequila as if a shipwreck of Homeric pro-
portions were occurring in the bottom of the glass,
which was, you have to admit, strange behavior for
a kid his age, not quite twenty-one.

Then the adventure began.

I saw it. I can testify. I was sitting at another

table, talking to a rookie journalist who wrote for the culture pages of a Mexico City newspaper, and I had just bought a drawing from Lilian Serpas, who, after making the sale, had smiled her most enigmatic smile (though the word *enigmatic* cannot even adumbrate that abyss of darkness) and disappeared into the night, and I was telling the journalist who Lilian Serpas was; I was telling him that the drawing was the work of her son; I was telling him the little I knew about that woman who used to make fleeting appearances in the bars and cafés along the Avenida Bucareli. And then, as I was talking, as Arturo contemplated putative whirlpools in his tequila at the next table, Ernesto San Epifanio walked across from the bar and sat down next to him, and for a moment I could see only their heads, their mops of shoulder-length hair (Arturo's was curly while Ernesto's was straight and much darker), and they talked for a while as the last night owls gradually vacated the Encrucidada Veracruzana, some suddenly in a hurry to be gone, shouting, Viva Mexico! from the doorway, and some so drunk they could hardly get up out of their seats.

Then I got up and went and stood beside them like the crystal statue I wanted to be when I was a girl, and I listened as Ernesto San Epifanio told a terrible story about the King of the Rent Boys in Colonia Guerrero, a guy known as the King, who had a monopoly on male prostitution in that picturesque and indeed charming neighborhood of the capital. The King had bought Ernesto's body, which meant, so our friend told us, that he now belonged to that monarch body and soul (which is what happens if you're reckless enough to let yourself be bought), and if he did not accede to his new owner's demands, the judgment and the wrath of the King would fall upon him and upon his family. Arturito listened to what Ernesto was telling him, and from time to time he lifted his head from the maelstrom of his tequila and looked into his friend's eyes as if wondering how Ernesto could have made such a dumb mistake, how he could have got himself into that mess. And as if Ernesto had read his mind, he said there comes a time in the life of every gay man in Mexico when he goes and makes an irredeemably dumb-ass mistake, and then he said that he had no one to help him, and that if things went on the way they were going he'd end up being a slave to the King of the Rent Boys in Colonia Guerrero. Then Arturito, the kid I had met when he was seventeen, said, And you want me to help you get out of this fucking mess? And Ernesto San Epifanio said, There's no fucking way out of it, but I wouldn't say no to some help. And Arturo said, What do you want me to do? Kill the King of the Rent Boys? And Ernesto San Epifanio said, I don't want you to kill anyone, I just want you to come with me and tell him to leave me alone, for good. And Arturo said, Why the fuck don't you tell him yourself? And Ernesto said, If I go on my own and tell him, all the King's heavies will beat me to a pulp and throw my body to the dogs. And Arturo said, What a fuck-up. And Ernesto San Epifanio said, But nobody fucks with you. And Arturo said, Don't fucking push it. And Ernesto said, Well I'm fucked already, my poems will go down in the martyrology of Mexican poetry. If you don't want to come with me, fine. In the end, you're right. Right about what? said Arturo, stretching as if he'd been asleep until that moment. Then they started talking about the power wielded by the King of the Rent Boys in Colonia Guerrero and Arturo asked what that power was based on. Fear, said Ernesto San Epifanio. The King ruled by fear. And what am I supposed to do? asked Arturo. You're not afraid, said Ernesto. You've just come back from Chile. Whatever the King can do to me, you've seen it multiplied a hundred times or a hundred thousand. I couldn't see Arturo's reaction but I guessed that the slightly vacant expression on his face until then was subtly unsettled by a small, almost imperceptible wrinkle, in which all the world's fear was concentrated. Then Arturito laughed and Ernesto laughed and in the ashen space of the Encrucijada Veracruzana at that late hour their crystalline peals of laughter were like polymorphic birds. Then Arturo got up and said, Let's go to Colonia Guerrero, and Ernesto got up and went out with him, and thirty seconds later I too deserted that moribund bar and followed them at a careful distance, because I knew that if they saw me, they wouldn't let me come along, because I was a woman and they were on men's business, because I was older and didn't have the vigor of a twenty-year-old, and because at that uncertain hour before dawn Arturito Belano was assuming his destiny as a child of the sewers and setting out to confront his ghosts.

But I didn't want to let him go on his own. Him or Ernesto San Epifanio. So I followed at a careful distance, and as I walked I felt in my bag or my old satchel from Oaxaca, looking for my lucky knife, and this time I found it straight away, and put it in a pocket of my pleated skirt, a grey pleated skirt it was, with pockets on both sides, a gift from Elena, which I rarely wore. And right then I didn't think about what I was doing and the consequences it could have for me or for the others who would no doubt be affected. I thought of Ernesto, who was wearing a lilac-colored jacket and a dark green shirt with stiff collar and cuffs, and I thought about the consequences of desire. And then I thought of Arturo, who had suddenly been promoted to the rank of revolutionary veteran and had, for some obscure reason best known to himself, accepted the responsibilities entailed by that error.

I followed them: I saw them go down Bucareli to Reforma with a spring in their step and then cross Reforma without waiting for the lights to change, their long hair blowing in the excess wind that funnels down Reforma at that hour of the night, turning it into a transparent tube or an elongated lung exhaling the city's imaginary breath. Then we walked down the Avenida Guerrero; they weren't stepping so lightly any more, and I wasn't feeling too enthusiastic either. Guerrero, at that time of night, is more like a cemetery than an avenue, not a cemetery in 1974 or in 1968, or 1975, but a cemetery in the year 2666, a forgotten cemetery under the eyelid of a corpse or an unborn child, bathed in the dispassionate fluids of an eye that tried so hard to forget one particular thing that it ended up forgetting everything else.

And by that stage we had already crossed the

Puente de Alvarado and glimpsed the last human ants making their way across the Plaza San Fernando under cover of darkness, and I began to feel seriously nervous because from that moment on we were venturing into the kingdom of the King of the Rent Boys, who had inspired such fear in the elegant Ernesto (a son of Mexico City's long-suffering working class, incidentally).

So there she was, my friends, the mother of Mexican poetry with a knife in her pocket, following two poets who still hadn't turned twenty-one down that turbulent river that was and is the Avenida Guerrero, comparable if not to the Amazon, for that would be an exaggeration, at least to the Grijalva, once honored by the song of Efraín Huerta (if I remember rightly), although the nocturnal Grijalva that is and was the Avenida Guerrero had long since lost its condition of original innocence, by which I mean that the urban version of the Grijalva, flowing in the night, was in every respect a damned river, a river of the damned, ferrying corpses and corpses-to-be, black automobiles that appeared, vanished, and then reappeared, the same ones or their silent, demented echoes, as if the river of Hell were circular, which, now I come to think of it, is probably the case.

Be that as it may, I followed them as they proceeded along the Avenida Guerrero and then turned down the Calle Magnolia, and to judge from their gestures they were having an animated conversation, although it was hardly the ideal time or place to engage in an exchange of views. From the bars still open on the Calle Magnolia (of which, admittedly, there were few) a wan tropical music emanated, more conducive to meditation than to festivity or dancing, punctuated from time to time by a resounding shout. I remember thinking that the street seemed to be a thorn or an arrow lodged in the side of the Avenida Guerrero, an image that Ernesto San Epifanio might have appreciated. Then they stopped in front of the Clover Hotel with its neon sign, which was funny, in a way, since it was like finding an establishment by the name of Paris in the Calle Berlin, or so it struck me at least (I was very nervous), and they seemed to be deliberating over what strategy to follow from that point on. I had the impression that, at the last minute, Ernesto wanted to turn around and get out of there as fast as possible, while Arturito was resolved to continue, having entirely assumed the role of hard man, which was partly my creation, and which, in the course of that helpless, airless night, he had accepted like a wafer of bitter flesh, the host that no one can be qualified to swallow.

Our two heroes went into the Clover Hotel: first Arturo Belano, followed by Ernesto San Epifanio, poets forged in the smithy of Mexico City, and then I, León Felipe's cleaning lady, breaker of Don Pedro Garfías's vases, the only person who remained in the UNAM in September 1968, when the riot police violated the autonomy of the university, I went in after them. And at first glance the interior of the hotel was a disappointment to me. At such moments you feel as if you were shutting your eyes and throwing yourself into a swimming pool of fire. I threw myself in. I opened my eyes. And there was nothing terrible about what I saw. A tiny lobby with two sofas unspeakably scarred by the passage of time, a short, swarthy man at the desk, with an enormous mass of jet-black hair, a fluorescent tube hanging from the ceiling, a green-tiled floor, a staircase covered with a dirty grey plastic runner, in short, a no-star lobby, although, for some of Colonia Guerrero's inhabitants, the Clover would perhaps have seemed a rather luxurious hotel.

After exchanging a few words with the receptionist, Arturo and Ernesto went up the stairs, then I came in and said that I was with them. The swarthy guy blinked. He was going to say something; he was going to play the guard dog, but I was already on the next floor, walking down a corridor bathed in sickly light, redolent of disinfectant and absolutely unadorned, as if its nakedness dated back to the first days of creation. I opened a door that had just been closed and stepped into my role as witness in the royal bed-chamber of the King of the Rent Boys in Colonia Guerrero.

I hardly need tell you, my friends, that the King was not alone.

In the room was a table, and on the table was a green cloth, but the occupants of the room were not playing cards; they were settling the day's or the week's accounts, and spread out on the green cloth were papers with names and numbers written on them, and money.

No one was surprised to see me.

The King was solidly built and he must have been about thirty years old. He had brown hair, that shade of brown that in Mexico they call *güero*, whether seriously or as a joke I've never been able to tell, and I guess I never will. He was wearing a slightly sweaty white shirt, which revealed, for all to see, a pair of muscular, hairy forearms. Next to him was sitting a chubby guy with a mustache and out-size sideburns, probably the chancellor of the king-dom. At the back of the room, on a bed in the shadows, a third man was watching and listening to us, moving his head. My first thought was that he was ill. At the start, he was the only one who fright-ened me, but as the minutes went by my fear gave way to pity: I realized that the man on the bed, in that semi-prostrate position (which can't have been easy to maintain), must have been an invalid, or maybe disabled, maybe the King's disabled or sedated nephew, which led me to reflect that how-ever bad one's situation (I was thinking of Ernesto San Epifanio), there's always somebody worse off.

I remember the King's words. I remember his smile when he saw Ernesto and his inquisitive look when he saw Arturo. I remember how the King set a distance between his person and his visitors sim-ply by gathering up the money and putting it into his pocket.

The King mentioned two nights during which Ernesto had willingly given himself and spoke of contracting obligations, the obligations implicit in every act, however gratuitous or accidental. He

ROBERTO BOLAÑO

spoke of the heart, a man's heart, which bleeds like
a woman (I think he was referring to menstruation)
and obliges a real man to take responsibility for
his acts, whatever they might be. And he spoke of
debts: there was nothing more despicable than a
badly paid debt. That's what he said. Not an unpaid
debt but a badly paid debt. Then he stopped talk-
ing and waited to hear what his visitors had to say.

The first to speak was Ernesto San Epifanio. He
said that he didn't owe any debt to the King. He
said that all he had done was to sleep with him
two nights in a row (two wild nights, he specified),
vaguely aware that he was going to bed with the
King of the Rent Boys, but without measuring the
dangers and "responsibilities" that such an act
entailed, in all innocence (although as he said the
word *innocence*, Ernesto couldn't stifle a giggle,
which was rather at odds with his self-exoneration),
guided only by desire and a sense of adventure, and
not by any secret plan of enslaving himself to the
King of the Rent Boys.

You are my fucking slave, said the King, inter-
rupting him. I am your fucking slave, said the man
or the boy at the back of the room. He had a high-
pitched, pained voice that gave me a start. The
King turned around and ordered him to be quiet.
I'm not your fucking slave, said Ernesto. The King

looked at Ernesto with a patient, malicious smile. He asked him who he thought he was. A Mexican homosexual poet, said Ernesto, a homosexual poet, a poet, a . . . (all this meant nothing to the King), and then he added something about his right (his *inalienable* right) to sleep with whoever he liked without having to become anybody's slave. This is crazy! If it wasn't so tragic I'd be killing myself, he said. Go ahead, then, before we get to work. The King's voice had suddenly gone hard. Ernesto blushed. I could see him in profile and I noticed that his lower lip was trembling. We're going to make you suffer, said the King. We're going to stick it to you, said the chancellor of the kingdom. We're going to beat you till your fucking lungs and heart explode, said the King. The strange thing, though, was that they said all this without moving their lips and without any sound coming out of their mouths.

Leave me alone, said Ernesto's etiolated voice.

The poor disabled boy at the back of the room started shaking and covered himself with a blanket. Soon we could all hear his stifled sobs.

Then Arturo spoke. Who's he? he asked.

Who's who, jerk? said the King. Who's that guy? said Arturo, pointing at the mass on the bed. The chancellor turned and looked inquisitively toward the back of the room, then looked at Arturo and Ernesto with an empty smile. The King did not turn around. Who is he? repeated Arturo. Who the fuck are *you*? said the King.

The boy at the back of the room shuddered under the blanket. He seemed to be turning around. He was tangled up or suffocating, and you couldn't tell if his head was near the pillow or down at the foot of the bed. He's sick, said Arturo. It wasn't a question, or even an affirmation. It was as if he were talking to himself, and, at the same time, losing his nerve, and weirdly, at that moment, when I heard him speak, instead of thinking about what he had said or about that poor sick boy, I noticed that Arturo's Chilean accent had returned during the months he had spent in his country (and he still hadn't lost it). Which made me wonder what would happen in the unlikely event that I went back to Montevideo. Would my accent come back? Would I gradually cease to be the mother of Mexican poetry? It was typical: for some reason, I always have absurd, outlandish thoughts at the worst moments.

And that was definitely one of the worst; it even occurred to me that the King could kill us with impunity, and throw our bodies to the dogs, the silent dogs of Colonia Guerrero, or do something worse still. But then Arturo cleared his throat (or that is what it sounded like to me), sat down on an empty chair in front of the King (a chair that hadn't been there before) and covered his face with his hands (as if he were dizzy or thought he might faint). The King and the chancellor of the kingdom looked at him curiously, as if they had never seen such a listless hit man in their lives. Then, with his face still in his hands, Arturo said that they had to sort out Ernesto San Epifanio's problems once and for all, then and there. The curious expression drained from the King's face, as curious expressions do: they are always on the point of morphing into something else. They drain away, but not entirely; traces remain, because curiosity is lasting, and although the voyage from indifference to curiosity can seem brief (because we are drawn on by a natural inclination) the return can feel interminable, like an unending nightmare. And it was clear from the King's gaze that he would have liked to escape from that nightmare through violence.

But then Arturo began to speak of other things. He spoke of the sick boy who was shivering on the bed at the back of the room, and said that we were going to take him with us. He spoke of death, and he spoke of the shivering boy, who had in fact stopped shivering by then and pulled back the edge of the blanket to peep out at us. He spoke of death, and repeated himself over and over, always going back to death, as if telling the King of the Rent Boys in Colonia Guerrero that he had no competency in matters of death, and at the time I thought: He's making this up, it's fiction, a story, none of this is true, and then, as if Arturo Belano had read my thoughts, he turned just a little, barely moving his shoulders, said, Give it to me, and held out the palm of his right hand.

And on the palm of his right hand I placed my open jackknife, and he said thank you and turned his back on me again. The King asked him if he'd been hitting the bottle. No, said Arturo, well maybe, but only a bit. Then the King asked him if Ernesto was his boy. And Arturo said yes, which proved that I was right: it was the storyteller talking, not the booze. Then the King went to get up, perhaps to bid us good night and show us the door, but Arturo said, Don't move, you son of a bitch, no one moves, you sit still and you keep your fucking hands on the table, and, surprisingly, the King and the chancellor did as he said. I think at that point Arturo realized that he had won, or at least won the first half of the fight, or the first round, but he must have also realized that if the fight went on he could still lose. In other words, if this was a two-round fight, he had a good chance, but if the fight went to ten, or twelve, or fifteen rounds, his chances would be dwarfed by the immensity of the kingdom. So he went right ahead and told Ernesto to go and see how the boy at the back of the room was doing. And Ernesto looked at him as if to say, Come on, buddy, don't push it, but since it wasn't the moment for equivocation, he obeyed. From the back of the room Ernesto said that the kid was pretty far gone. I saw Ernesto. I saw him walk across the royal bedchamber, tracing an arc, until he reached the bed, where he uncovered the young slave and touched him, or perhaps gave him a pinch on the arm, whispered some words in his ear, put his own ear to the boy's lips, swallowed (I saw him swallow his saliva as he leaned across that swamp-like, desert-like bed), and said that the kid was pretty far gone. If this kid dies on us, I'm coming back to kill you, said Arturo. Then I opened my mouth for the first time that night: Are we going to take him with us, I asked. He's coming with us, said Arturo. And Ernesto, who was still at the back of the room, sat down on the bed, as if suddenly overcome by despondency, and said, Come and have a look yourself, Arturo. And I saw Arturo shake his head a number of times. He didn't want to see for himself. Then I looked at Ernesto and for a moment it seemed to me that the back of the room was sailing away from the rest of the building, with the bed as its taut sail, pulling away from the Clover Hotel, gliding off over a lake that was sailing in turn through a clear, clear sky, a sky from one of Dr. Atl's paintings of the valley of Mexico. The vision was so clear, all it needed was for Arturo and me to stand up and wave goodbye. And Ernesto seemed braver than ever to me. And the sick boy seemed brave too, in his way.

I moved. First mentally. Then physically. The sick boy looked me in the eyes and started to cry. He really was in a terrible state, but I thought it better not to tell Arturo. Where are his pants? Arturo asked. Somewhere around, said the King. I looked under the bed. There was nothing. I looked on both sides. I looked at Arturo as if to say, I can't find them, what should we do? Then Ernesto thought of looking among the blankets and he pulled out a pair of pants that looked damp and a pair of good tennis shoes. Leave it to me, I said. I sat the boy up on the edge of the bed and put on his jeans and his shoes. Then I lifted him up to see if he could walk. He could. Let's go, I said. Arturo didn't move. Wake up, Arturo, I thought. I have one more story to tell His Majesty, he said. You get going and wait for me at the front door.

Ernesto and I got the boy down the stairs. We hailed a taxi and waited at the entrance to the Clover Hotel. Shortly afterward, Arturo emerged. My recollections of that night when anything could have happened, but nothing did, are fragmentary, as if mauled by an enormous animal. Sometimes, thinking back, I can see a big thunderstorm moving in from the north toward the center of Mexico City, but my memory tells me that there was no thunderstorm that night, although the high Mexican sky did descend a little, and at times it was hard to breathe; the air was dry and it caught in the throat. I remember Ernesto San Epifanio and Arturo Belano laughing in the taxi, laughing their way back to reality or what they liked to think of as reality, and I remember the air as we stood on the sidewalk in front of the hotel and then inside the taxi, a cactus air, bristling with every one of Mexico's countless species of cactus, and I remember saying, It's hard to breathe, and, Give me back my knife, and, It's hard to talk, and, Where are we going. I remember that every time I spoke, Ernesto and Arturo burst out laughing, and I ended up laughing too, as much as them or more, we all laughed, all except the taxi driver, who at one point looked at us as if we were just like all the other clients he had picked up that night (which, given that this was Mexico City, would not have been at all unusual), and the sick boy, who had fallen asleep with his head on my shoulder.

And that was how we entered and left the kingdom of the King of the Rent Boys, an enclave in the wasteland of Colonia Guerrero, Ernesto San Epifanio, aged twenty or nineteen, a homosexual poet born in Mexico (and one of the two best poets of his generation, the other being Ulises Lima, who we didn't know at that stage), Arturo Belano, aged twenty, a heterosexual poet born in Chile, Juan de Dios Montes (also known as Juan de Dos Montes and Juan Dedos), aged eighteen, apprenticed to a baker in Colonia Buenavista, apparently bisexual, and myself, Auxilio Lacouture, of definitively indefinite age, reader and mother, born in Uruguay or the Eastern Republic, if you prefer, and witness to the intricate conduits of dryness.

And since I shall have no more to say about Juan de Dios Montes, I can at least tell you that his nightmare came to a good end.

For a few days he lived at Arturito's place, then he drifted from one rooftop room to another. In the end a group of us found him a job at a bakery in Colonia Roma and he disappeared from our lives, or so it seemed. He liked to get high sniffing glue. He was melancholic and glum. He was stoic.

One day I ran into him by chance in the Parque Hundido. I said, How are you, Juan de Dios. Real good, he answered. Months later, at the party that Ernesto threw when he was awarded the Salvador Novo fellowship (Arturo wasn't there—they had fallen out, as poets do), I said that on the night of our adventure (it already seemed so long ago), the life in danger hadn't been his, as we had all thought, but Juan's. Yes, said Ernesto, that's the conclusion I've come to as well. It was Juan de Dios who was going to die.

Our hidden purpose had been to stop him from being killed.

After that I came back to the world. I've had it with adventures, I said in a tiny little voice. Adventures, adventures. I had known the adventures of poetry, which are always matters of life and death, but when I came back to the streets of Mexico, I was content with everyday life. Why ask for more? Why go on fooling myself? The everyday is like a frozen transparency that lasts only a few seconds. So I came back and saw it and let it envelop me. I am the mother, I told it, and honestly I don't think I'm cut out for horror movies. Then the everyday began to expand like a soap bubble gone crazy, and popped.

I was back in the women's bathroom on the fourth floor of the Faculty of Philosophy and Literature and it was September 1968 and I was thinking about the adventures of Remedios Varo. There are so few people left who remember Remedios Varo. I never met her. I would sincerely love to be able to say that I'd met her, but the truth is that I never did. I have known marvelous women, strong as mountains or ocean currents, but I never met Remedios Varo. Not because I was too timid to pay her a visit at her house, not because I didn't admire her work (which I admire wholeheartedly), but because Remedios Varo died in 1963, and in 1963 I was still living in my beloved, faraway Montevideo.

Although some nights, when the moon shines into the women's bathroom and I am still awake, I think, No, in 1963, I was already in Mexico City and Don Pedro Garfías is listening distractedly as I ask him for Remedios Varo's address. Although the Catalan painter is not a particular friend of his, he knows and respects her, so he walks somewhat unsteadily to his desk, takes a slip of paper, a diary from a drawer, a fountain pen from his jacket pocket, and ceremoniously copies out the address in his beautiful handwriting.

So off I go flying to Remedios Varo's house, which is in Colonia Polanco, isn't it? Or Colonia Anzures, perhaps, or Colonia Tlaxpana? Memory plays malicious tricks on me when the light of the waning moon creeps into the women's bathroom like a spider. In any case, I rush headlong through the streets of Mexico City, which flash past, changing as I approach her house (each change building on the one that went before, each a sequel and a reproach), until I reach a street where all the houses seem to be ruined castles, and then I ring a doorbell and wait a few seconds, during which all I can hear is my heart beating (because I'm silly like that—when I'm about to meet someone I admire, my heart starts racing) and then I hear faint steps and someone opens the door and it is Remedios Varo.

She is fifty-four years old. Which means that she has a year left to live.

She invites me in. I don't have many visitors, she says. I walk in and she follows me. Go in, go in, she says, and I proceed down a feebly illuminated corridor to a large sitting room with two windows facing an interior courtyard, their heavy, lilac curtains drawn. In the sitting room there is an armchair, in which I sit down. There are two cups of coffee on a small round table. I notice three butts in an ashtray. The obvious conclusion is that there is a third person in the house. Remedios Varo looks me in the eye and smiles: I'm alone, she declares.

I say how much I admire her, I talk about the French surrealists and the Catalan surrealists, the Spanish Civil War, I don't mention Benjamin Péret because they parted in 1942, and I don't know on what terms, but I talk about Paris and exile, her arrival in Mexico and her friendship with Leonora Carrington, and then I realize that I am telling Remedios Varo the story of her life, I'm behaving like a nervous schoolgirl reciting her lesson for a non-existent board of examiners. And then I go red as a tomato and say, Sorry, I don't know what I say, I say, Do you mind if I smoke? and I look for my pack of Delicados in my satchel, but I can't find it, so I say, Do you have a cigarette? And Remedios Varo, who is standing with her back to a picture, a picture covered with an old skirt (but that old skirt, it occurs to me, must have belonged to a giant), says that she has given up smoking, that her lungs are delicate now, and although she doesn't look like she has bad lungs, or has even seen anything bad in her life, I know that she has seen many bad things, the ascension of the devil, the unstoppable procession of termites climbing the Tree of Life, the conflict between the Enlightenment and the Shadow or the Empire or the Kingdom of Order, which are all proper names for the irrational stain that is bent on turning us into beasts or robots, and which has been fighting against the Enlightenment since the beginning of time (a conjecture of mine, which the official representatives of the Enlightenment would no doubt reject), I know that she has seen things that very few women *know* they have seen, and now she is seeing her own death, which is set to occur in less than twelve months' time, and I know that there is someone else in her house who smokes and does not want to be discovered by me, which makes me think that whoever it is, it must be someone I know.

Then I sigh and look at the reflection of the waning moon in the tiles of the fourth-floor women's bathroom, and, overcoming weariness and fear, I raise my hand, point at the picture behind the giant skirt, and ask her, What is it? Remedios Varo smiles at me, then turns around; she turns her back on me and for a while she examines the picture, but without removing or drawing aside the skirt that shelters it from prying eyes. It's the last one, she says. Or maybe she says, It's the second-to-last one. Her words reverberate off the tiles scored by moonlight, so the *second* might have been smothered by an echo. And in that phase of radical insomnia I see all of Remedios Varo's pictures passing one after another like tears cried by the moon or my blue eyes. So, honestly, it's hard to notice details or distinguish clearly between *last* and *second-to-last*. And then Remedios Varo lifts up the giant's skirt to reveal an enormous valley, viewed from the highest mountain, a green and brown valley, and the mere sight of that landscape makes me anxious, because I know, just as I know there is another person in the house, that what the painter is showing me is a prelude, the setting for a scene that will be scorched into my soul, or no, not scorched, since nothing can affect me like that any more, what I sense is more like the approach of an ice man, a man made of ice cubes, who will come and kiss me on the mouth, on my toothless mouth, and I shall feel those lips of ice on my lips, and I will see those eyes of ice a few inches away from mine, and then I shall faint like Juana de Ibarbourou, and I will murmur, Why me? (a coquetry for which I shall be forgiven) and the man made of ice cubes will blink, and in that blink of an eye, I shall catch the briefest glimpse of a blizzard, as if someone had opened a window and then, on second thought, shut it again suddenly, saying, No, you shall see what you must, Auxilio, but all in good time.

I know that the landscape, the enormous valley,

vaguely reminiscent of a Renaissance background, is *waiting*.

But what is it waiting for?

And then Remedios Varo covers the canvas with the skirt and offers me a cup of coffee and we start talking about other things, aspects of daily life, although words from a different kind of context find their way into our conversation, like *parousia* or *hierophant*, like *psychotropic drugs* and *electroshock therapy*. And then we talk about someone who recently went on a hunger strike, and I hear myself saying, After a week without food, you don't feel hungry anymore, and Remedios Varo looks at me and says, You poor thing.

Just at that moment the heavy lilac curtain stirs and I leap to my feet and I can't (and won't) think about what the Catalan painter has just said. I go to the window, draw the curtain aside and discover a black kitten. I heave a sigh of relief. I know that behind me Remedios Varo is smiling and wondering who I am. The window gives onto a little courtyard with a garden where five or six other cats are taking a siesta. So many cats! Are they all yours? More or less, says Remedios Varo. I turn to look at her: the kitten is in her arms and she is saying, in Catalan: *There you are, sweetie. Where were you? I've been looking for you for hours.*

Would you like to listen to some music?

Is she talking to me or to the kitten? Me, I suppose, because she talks to the kitten in Catalan, although it's clear at a glance, to anyone, that the kitten is Mexican born and bred, from a line of Mexican stray cats going back at least three hundred years, and now that the moon is stealing from one bathroom tile to another with delicate feline steps, I ask myself if there were cats in Mexico before the Spanish came, and I answer in a dispassionate, objective, and even slightly indifferent manner, No, there were no cats; the cats came with the second or third wave of Europeans. And then, speaking like a sleepwalker, because I am thinking about the sleepwalking cats of Mexico, I reply, Yes, and Remedios Varo goes to the record player, an old record player, which is not at all surprising since we are in the incredible year 1962 and everything is old, everything raises a hand to its mouth as I do to stifle a cry of surprise or an untimely confession, and she puts on a record and says, It's the Concertino in A minor by Salvador Bacarisse, and, listening to that Spanish music for the first time, I begin to cry, again, while the moon jumps from one tile to another in slow motion, as if I and not nature were directing this film.

How much time do we spend listening to Bacarisse?

I don't know. All I know is that at some point Remedios Varo lifts the arm of the record player and brings the listening to an end. And then I go to her (I have to admit it, I don't want to leave) and, blushing deeply, I offer to wash the cups we used, to sweep the floor, to dust her furniture, to scour the pots and pans in her kitchen, to go out and do the shopping, to make the bed or run a bath, but Remedios Varo smiles and says, I don't need you to do any of that, Auxilio, but thanks anyway. I'm fine, really. I don't need any help. As she shows me to the front door I think, Liar! How can she not need any help?

And then I see myself in the hallway of her house. She is inside with her hand on the door-handle. There are so many things I would like to ask her. For a start, if I can visit her again. Now the whole street is awash with sunlight like white wine. That sunlight illuminates her face and tinges it with a brave melancholy. Fine. Everything is fine. It's time for me to go. I don't know whether to shake her hand or kiss her on both cheeks. Latin American women, as far as I know, give just the one kiss. On one cheek. Spanish women give two. And

French women three. When I was a girl I used to think that the three kisses stood for Liberty, Equality, and Fraternity. Now I know they don't, but I still like to think they do. So I give her three kisses and she looks at me as if she too, at some point, had shared my theory. A kiss on the left cheek, one on the right, and a final kiss on the left. And Remedios Varo looks at me and her eyes say, Don't worry, Auxilio, you're not going to die, you're not going to go crazy, you're upholding academic independence, you're defending the honor of our American universities, at worst you might become terribly thin, or have visions, or they might even find you, but don't think about that, be strong, read poor old Pedrito Garfías (you could at least have brought something else to read, you silly girl!) and let your mind flow freely through time, from the 18th to the 30th of September 1968, not one day more, that's all you have to do.

And then, as Remedios Varo shuts the door, she darts a last gaze straight into my eyes, and it is implacably clear to me that she is dead.

TEN

I left Remedios Varo's house like a sleepwalker, but even more lost, because sleepwalkers always find their way back, and I knew that I would never return to that house. I knew that I would wake up shelterless, at night or as the day was breaking, not that it mattered, somewhere in the heart of the city that love or rage had led me to choose.

And now my memories, wandering without rhyme or reason backward and forwards from that helpless month of September 1968 mumble and stutter and tell me that I decided to stay there and wait in that watery sunlight, standing on a corner, listening to all the sounds of Mexico City, down to the sound of architectural shadows pursuing one another like wild animals sprung from a taxidermist's lair.

My senses held me pinned in a purely spatial world, so I couldn't say whether a long or a short span of time elapsed before I saw the door of Remedios Varo's house open and a woman come out, the one who had been hiding in the bedroom or the bathroom or behind the curtains during my visit.

A woman who, although she had long slim legs, was inferior to me in stature, I reckoned as I followed her. Because although the woman was tall, especially by Mexican standards, I was taller still.

Tailing her, I could see only her back and legs. She was slimly built, as I said, with a head of brown, slightly wavy hair falling below her shoulders, hair which, in spite of a certain disarray (which could have been taken for scruffiness, though I wouldn't dare call it that), was not without grace.

Everything about her, in fact her whole person, gave off a kind of grace, though it was hard to tell exactly why, since she was dressed in a sober and

unexceptional manner, and there was nothing par-
ticularly original about her clothing: a black skirt
and a cream-colored cardigan, both very worn, of
the kind that can be bought for a few pesos from a
market stall. Oddly, however, she was wearing
high-heeled shoes, not very high heels, but dressy
all the same, shoes that really didn't match the rest
of her attire. She was carrying a folder full of papers
under her arm.

Instead of waiting at the bus stop, as I'd thought
she would, she kept walking toward the center of
the city. After a while she went into a café. I stayed
outside and watched her through the front win-
dow. I saw her approach a table, take something
out of the folder and display it: one sheet, then
another. They were drawings, or reproductions of
drawings. The man and the woman sitting at the
table looked at the papers and then shook their
heads. She smiled at them and then proceeded to
the next table, where the scene was repeated. The
result was the same. Undeterred, she went to
another table, then another and another, until she
had approached them all. She sold one drawing.
For just a few coins, which made me think that it
was a buyer's market. Then she went to the bar,
where she exchanged a few words with a waitress.
She spoke and the waitress listened. They probably

knew each other. When the waitress turned around to make a coffee, she took the opportunity to engage the men at the bar in conversation and try to make a sale, but this time she spoke without moving from her place and one or maybe two men came over to where she was and glanced idly at her treasures.

She must have been about sixty. And she certainly looked it. Maybe she was older. And this happened ten years after the death of Remedios Varo, that is, in 1973, not 1963.

Then a chill ran down my spine. And the chill said to me: Hey, Auxilio (with an Uruguayan, not a Mexican, accent), the woman you're following, the woman who slipped out of Remedios Varo's house, she's the real mother of Mexican poetry, not you; this woman whose footsteps you are following, she's the mother, not you, not you, not you.

I think my head began to ache and I shut my eyes. I think the teeth I no longer had began to ache and I shut my eyes. And when I opened them she was at the bar, absolutely alone, sitting on a stool, drinking coffee with milk and reading a magazine that she probably kept in the folder, along with the reproductions of her beloved son's drawings.

A couple of yards away, the waitress had her elbows on the bar and her gaze fixed dreamily on

an indefinite point outside the windows, some-
where over my head. Some of the tables had been
vacated. At others, people were getting back to
their own business.

Then I realized that the woman I had been fol-
lowing, whether awake or in a dream, was Lilian
Serpas, and I remembered her story, or what little I
knew of it.

For a time, in the fifties I guess, Lilian had been
a reasonably well-known poet and a woman of
extraordinary beauty. The origin of her family
name is unclear; it sounds Greek (to me, anyway),
or Hungarian, maybe, it could even be an old
Castilian name. But Lilian was Mexican and she
had lived almost all her life in Mexico City. It was
said that in the course of her drawn-out youth she
had many fiancés and admirers. Lilian, however,
was not interested in fiancés, she wanted lovers,
and she had them too.

I would've liked to say to her: Lilian, you don't
need so many lovers, they'll use you up and dump
you on a street corner, what else can you expect
from men? But what did I know, I was just some
crazy virgin, and Lilian led her sex life as she
pleased, intensely, guided only by her own bodily
pleasure and the pleasure of the sonnets she was
writing at the time. And, of course, it didn't turn

out well for her. Or maybe it did. Who am I to say? She had lovers. I've had hardly any.

Anyhow, one day, Lilian fell in love with a man and had a child with him. The guy was called Coffeen, he might have been North American, or maybe he was English, or Mexican. In any case she had a child with him and the name of the child was Carlos Coffeen Serpas. The painter Carlos Coffeen Serpas.

At some point (I don't know exactly when), Mr. Coffeen disappeared. Maybe he left Lilian. Maybe Lilian left him. Maybe it was more romantic: Coffeen died and Lilian wanted to die as well, but she survived for the sake of the child. And soon there were new admirers to console her, because Lilian was still beautiful and she still liked going to bed with men and moaning with pleasure till daybreak. Meanwhile young Coffeen Serpas was growing up; at an early age, he was introduced to the circles in which his mother moved, and everyone was amazed by his intelligence and convinced that he would have a brilliant career in the treacherous world of art.

And who else moved in those circles, along with Lilian Serpas and her son? The same old crowd: the old, failed journalists and Spanish exiles who used to gather in the bars and cafés of downtown

Mexico City. Very friendly people but not exactly ideal company for a sensitive child, in my opinion.

In those years Lilian held a series of different jobs. She worked as a secretary, and as a sales assistant in various boutiques; for a time she was employed by a couple of newspapers and even by a two-bit radio station. These stints never lasted very long, because, as she told me, not without a certain sadness, when you're a poet and you have to live by night, there's no way you can hold down a steady job.

Of course I understood, and I agreed with her, although even as I expressed my agreement, my voice and my body language automatically and unconsciously betrayed an attitude of sickening superiority, as if I were saying to her, Sure, Lilian, that's fine, but in the end isn't it all a bit childish? Sure, it's enjoyable and amusing, but don't count on me to help carry out your experiment.

As if splitting my time between the deleterious Avenida Bucareli and the university made me any better. As if knowing and associating with young poets as well as old, failed journalists made me any better. The truth is, I'm no better. The truth is, young poets usually end up as old, failed journalists. And the university, my beloved university is lurking in the sewers underneath the Avenida

Bucareli, waiting for its day to come.

One night, Lilian told me this herself, she met an exiled South American at the Café Quito and talked with him until closing time. Then they went to Lilian's apartment and climbed into bed without making a sound so as not to wake young Carlos Coffeen. The South American was Ernesto Guevara. I don't believe you, Lilian, I said to her. It's true, it was him, said Lilian, in that peculiar voice she had when I met her: brittle, the voice of a broken doll, the sort of voice Cervantes' glass graduate would have had, if he'd been a woman, that is, and taken leave of his senses while remaining perfectly lucid, back in the hapless Golden Age of Spanish Literature. And what was Che Guevara like in bed, was the first thing I wanted to know. Lilian said something I couldn't hear. What? I said. What? What? Normal, said Lilian, staring at the creased surface of her folder.

Maybe it was a lie. When I met Lilian, the only thing she seemed to care about was selling reproductions of her son's drawings. Poetry left her cold. She would turn up at the Café Quito very late and sit down at a table with the young poets, or with the old, failed journalists (all of whom had slept with her) and pass the time listening to the same old conversations. If someone said, for example,

Tell us about Che Guevara, she would say, He was normal. That was all. As it happened, a number of those failed journalists had known Che Guevara and Fidel during their stay in Mexico, and no one was surprised to hear Lilian say that the Che was normal, although perhaps they didn't know that Lilian had actually *slept* with him; they thought she had slept only with them and a few bigwigs who didn't frequent the Avenida Bucareli in the small hours of the morning, no one really special, in other words.

I admit I would have liked to know what Che Guevara was like in bed. So he was normal, OK, but normal how?

One night I challenged Lilian, saying, These kids have a right to know exactly what Che was like in bed. One of my crazier declarations, but I went ahead and made it anyway.

I remember Lilian looking at me with her pained, wrinkled doll's mask, which seemed to be perpetually on the point of dropping to reveal the Queen of the Seas with her cohorts of thunder, yet always remained lifeless. These kids, she said, these kids, and then looked up at the ceiling of the Café Quito, which was being painted by two youths perched on a mobile scaffold.

That's what she was like, the woman I followed

from the dream of Remedios Varo, the great Catalan painter, to the dream of Mexico City's incurable streets, where something was always happening, while seeming to whisper or shout or hiss at you: Nothing ever happens here.

So there I am once again at the Café Quito in 1973 or maybe the first months of '74; it's eleven o'clock and through the smoke, lit as if by tracer fire, I see Lilian arrive enveloped, as always, in smoke, and her smoke and that of the café eye each other like spiders before coalescing into a single coffee-scented cloud (there's a roaster in the Café Quito, and it's one of the few places on the Avenida Bucareli that has an Italian espresso machine).

Then the young poets of Mexico, my friends, greet her without getting up from their table. They say, Good evening, Lilian Serpas, or, What's up, Lilian Serpas? Even the most addled pronounce some kind of greeting, as if by so doing they could make a goddess descend from the heights of the Café Quito (where two intrepid young painters are at work, balanced in a fashion I can only describe as precarious) and award them The Order of Poetic Merit, when in reality what they are doing (but this is a thought I keep to myself) by greeting her in that manner is placing their addled young heads on the chopping block.

And Lilian stops, as if she didn't hear properly, and looks for the table where they are sitting (I am sitting there too) and, having spotted us, comes over to say hello and to see if she can perhaps sell one of her reproductions, and I look the other way.

Why do I look the other way?

Because I know her story.

So I look the other way while Lilian, standing or seated, says hello to each of them in turn, the five or often more motley young poets around that table, and when she gets to me, I look up from the ground, turn my head so slowly it's exasperating (but I really can't turn it any faster) and, compliantly, reply to her greeting.

And time goes by (in the end Lilian doesn't try to sell us any drawings because she knows we don't have any money and wouldn't buy them anyway, but if anyone wants to take a look, she's happy to show them the reproductions, which are of surprisingly high quality, printed with a proper press on glossy paper, which reveals something about the curious business sense of Carlos Coffeen Serpas or of his mother, mendicant entrepreneurs who, in a moment of inspiration that I would rather not try to imagine, decided to live exclusively from the proceeds of art) and gradually people start to leave or change tables, since, at the Café Quito, after a certain time of night, everyone knows everyone else, more or less, and everyone wants to have a chat or at least exchange a few words with his or her acquaintances. So there I am, stranded in the midst of that ceaseless mingling, staring at my half-empty coffee cup, when suddenly (it's almost like a cut to a new scene) an evasive shadow, so evasive it seems to attract all the other shadows in the café, as if it could exert a gravitational force on absences of light, approaches my table and sits down next to me.

How are you doing, Auxilio? says the ghost of Lilian Serpas.

Fine, just hanging out, I say.

And that is when time stands still again, a worn-out image if ever there was one, because either time never stands still or it has always been standing still; so let's say instead that a tremor disturbs the continuum of time, or that time plants its big feet wide apart, bends down, puts its head between its legs, looking at me upside down, one eye winking crazily just a few inches below its ass, or let's say that the full or waxing or obscurely waning moon of Mexico City slides again over the tiles of the women's bathroom on the fourth floor of the Faculty of Philosophy and Literature, or that the silence of a wake falls over the Café Quito and all I can hear are the murmurs of Lilian Serpas's ghostly court and once again I don't know if I'm in 1968 or 1974 or 1980, or gliding, finally, like the shadow of a sunken ship, toward the blessed year 2000, which I shall not live to see.

Be that as it may, something is happening as time passes. I know that time and not, for example, space, is making something happen. Something that has happened before, although in a sense every time is the first time so experience counts for nothing, which is better in the end, because experience is generally a hoax.

And then Lilian (the only one who emerges from this story unscathed, since she has already been through it all) asks me, once again, to do her a favor, the first and last favor she will ask of me in her life.

She says, It's late. She says, You're so pretty, Auxilio. She says, I often think of you, Auxilio. And I look at her and I look at the ceiling of the Café Quito, where the two sleepy young men are still working or pretending to work, perched on the most precarious scaffolding, and then I look back at Lilian: she's talking to me but staring at the large chunky glass containing her coffee with milk. With one ear I'm listening to what she's saying, and with the other to the Café Quito regulars kidding the youths on the scaffolding, yelling remarks that are, I gather, part of some masculine initiation rite, supposedly affectionate but in fact foreshadowing a disaster that will engulf not only the pair of broadbrush painters (or plumbers or electricians, I don't know, I just saw them there, and I can see them still, as the moonlight makes its crazy way over every tile in the women's bathroom, as if its course—and this is a terrifying thought—exhausted all the possibilities of subversion), a disaster that will engulf not just the painters but the jeerers as well, the givers of advice, in other words: us.

And then Lilian says, You have to go to my place. She says, I can't go home tonight. She says, You have to go and tell Carlos I'll be back early tomorrow morning. And my first impulse is to refuse point blank. But then Lilian looks me in the face and smiles at me (she doesn't cover her mouth when she speaks, like me, or when she smiles, although she should) and I am at a loss for words because I am looking at the mother of Mexican poetry, the worst mother Mexican poetry could possibly have, but its one, true mother none the less. So I say yes, I will go to her apartment if she gives me the address and if it's not too far away, and I will tell Carlos Coffeen, the painter, that his mother will be staying out all night.

And I see myself that night, my friends, walking toward Lilian Serpas's apartment, driven by a mystery that is, intermittently, like the wind of Mexico City, a black wind full of geometrically shaped holes, and at other moments more like the city's calm, an obeisant calm whose sole property is that of being a mirage.

You might be surprised to learn that I didn't know Carlos Coffeen Serpas. No one did, really. Or to be precise, a few people knew him, and they had

ROBERTO BOLAÑO

hatched the legend, the minor legend of a crazy painter who never left his mother's apartment, an apartment that, in some versions, was endowed with massive, dusty furniture that could have been buried in the crypt of one of the Emperor Maximilian's followers, although, according to other accounts, mother and son lived in something more like a tenement building, a faithful reproduction of the Burrón family's apartment (ah, the invincible Burrón family, God bless them, long may their comic strip run; when I arrived in Mexico, the first guy who tried to chat me up said I was the spitting image of Borola Tacuche, which isn't too far from the truth). The reality, as it sadly tends to be, was halfway between these imaginary extremes: neither crumbling palace nor tenement house, but an old four-story building in the Calle República de El Salvador, near the church of San Felipe Neri.

Carlos Coffeen Serpas was more than forty years old, and no one I knew had seen him for a long time. What did I think of his drawings? I didn't like them much, to be perfectly honest. Figures, almost always very thin, and sickly-looking too: that was what he used to draw. Flying or buried figures, sometimes staring out into the eyes of the viewer, and usually gesturing in some way. For example, holding a finger to their lips to request silence. Or covering their eyes. Or holding up an open, unlined hand. That's all I can say. I don't know much about art.

Anyway, there I was, in front of the gate of Lilian's building, and while I was thinking about her son's drawings, which probably had the distinction of being the cheapest on the Mexican art market, I was also thinking about what I would say to Coffeen when he opened the door to me.

Lilian lived on the top floor. I rang the bell a number of times. No one answered and for a moment I thought that Coffeen Serpas must be in some bar nearby, because he was reputed to be an incorrigible alcoholic. I was about to leave when something, I couldn't say exactly what, an intuition possibly, or perhaps just my natural curiosity, exacerbated by the time of night and by having walked all that way, prompted me to cross the street and take up a position on the opposite sidewalk. The lights in the windows on the fourth floor were out, but after a few seconds I thought I saw a curtain move, as if the wind that wasn't blowing through the streets of Mexico City was being channeled through the interior of that darkened apartment. And that was too much for me.

I crossed the street and rang the bell again. Then, without waiting for the door to open, I went back to the opposite sidewalk, watched the windows, and saw a curtain being drawn back. This time I could see a shadow, the silhouette of a man looking down at me, knowing that I could see him, not seeming to care anymore, and then I knew that the shadow was Carlos Coffeen Serpas, looking at me and wondering who I was, what I was doing there at that hour of night, what I wanted, what abhorrent news I was bearing.

For a moment I was sure he wouldn't open the door to me. It was common knowledge that Lilian's son was a complete recluse. Not that anyone wanted to visit him. So it was an odd situation, whichever way you looked at it.

I waved to him.

Then, lowering my gaze, I crossed the street for the fourth or fifth time, pretending as best I could to be confident. After a few seconds, the door opened with a click that echoed in the entrance hall. I climbed warily up to the fourth floor. The staircase was dimly lit. On the fourth-floor landing, Carlos Coffeen Serpas was waiting for me behind a door left ajar.

I don't know why I didn't just say what I had to say to him, then turn around and go home. Coffeen was tall, taller than his mother, and you could tell that in his youth he must have been slim and well built, although now he was fat, or, rather, bloated. His forehead was broad, but it didn't have the sort of breadth that suggests intelligence or sound judgment; it had the breadth of a battlefield, and the battle had been lost, to judge from the rest of his face: thin, lank hair falling over his ears, a skull more like a dented bowl than a noble dome, light eyes staring at me with a mixture of suspicion and boredom. In spite of everything, I found him attractive (I'm a born optimist).

I'm so tired, I said to him. After looking at me for a few seconds without inviting me in, he asked who I was. I'm a friend of Lilian's, I said. My name is Auxilio Lacouture and I work at the university.

At the time, in fact, I wasn't doing any kind of work at the university. In other words, I was unemployed again. But, faced with Coffeen, I thought it would be more reassuring to say I had a job at the faculty than to confess that I was out of work. Reassuring for whom? Well, for both of us: for me, because it gave me some kind of imaginary status or backing, and for him, because it meant he wasn't being visited late at night by a slightly younger double of his dear, dreadful mother. It's not something to be proud of. I know. But that's what I said, and then I looked him straight in the eye and waited for him to stand aside.

Coffeen had no choice but to ask me if I would like to come in, like a sullen boy receiving a surprise visit from his girlfriend. Of course I wanted to come in. So in I went and saw what lights remained in Lilian's apartment. A small entrance hall full of packages: reproductions of her son's drawings. And then a short, dark passage leading to a room where there was no hiding the poverty in which the ex-poet and the ex-painter lived. But I don't turn up my nose at poverty. In Latin America no one is ashamed of being poor (except perhaps some Chileans). There was, however, something abysmal about this poverty: entering Lilian's apartment was like plunging into the depths of an Atlantic trench. There, in deceptive stillness, the intruder was observed by the charred, mossy or plankton-covered remains of what had once been a life, a family, a mother and son, a real son, not invented or adopted like those prodigal sons of mine; a subtle inventory or anti-inventory of traces, emanating from the walls, speaking in a murmur like the voice of a black hole about Lilian's lovers, Carlitos Coffeen Serpas at primary school, the breakfasts and the dinners, the nightmares and the daylight that came in when Lilian drew the curtains, curtains that looked filthy now, curtains that a housework addict like myself would have taken down immediately and washed by hand in the kitchen sink, if I hadn't been afraid that any sudden movement on my part might have hardened the painter's gaze, which was gradually becoming milder as I let the seconds pass in silence, as if he had provisionally accepted my presence there in his last redoubt.

And that's all I can say. I wanted to stay; I kept still and quiet. But my eyes took in everything: the sofa sagging down to the floor, the low table covered with papers, napkins and dirty glasses, Coffeen's dust-covered paintings hanging on the walls, the hallway making its rash, inexorable way toward the mother's room, the son's room and the bathroom, which is where I went, having asked permission, having waited for Coffeen to deliberate with himself or with Coffeen 2 or perhaps even Coffeen 3, the bathroom, which was comparable in every respect to the living room, and which, as I walked down that dark passage (all the passages in Lilian's apartment were dark), I imagined as lacking a mirror, mistakenly, because there *was* a mirror there, perfectly normal in size and placement, over the small sink, and after having a pee, I took another good look at myself in the mercury of that mirror, at my thin face, blond page-boy hair and toothless smile, because there, my friends, there in Lilian Serpas's bathroom, a room that had probably not been graced for many years by the presence of a visitor, I found myself thinking about happiness, just like that, the happiness possibly hidden under the crusts of filth in that apartment, and when you're happy or sense that happiness may be imminent you're not afraid to look at yourself in mirrors, indeed, when you're happy or feel predestined for happiness, you tend to lower your guard and face up to mirrors, out of curiosity, I guess, or because you're feeling good in your skin, as the Frenchified citizens of Montevideo used to say (may God grant them some remnant of health). So I looked at myself in Lilian and Coffeen's bathroom mirror and I saw Auxilio Lacouture, and what I saw, my friends, moved my soul in contradictory ways, since, on one hand, it could have made me laugh, what I was seeing so clearly there: my skin slightly ruddy from fatigue and alcohol, but my eyes quite wide open (when I go without sleep, my eyes become two cashbox slots collecting not the sadly hoped-for coins of my chimerical savings but coins of fire from a future blaze in which nothing makes any sense), eyes wide open, shining and awake, ideal eyes for appreciating a nocturnal exhibition of Carlos Coffeen's work, but, on the other hand, I also saw my lips, my poor little lips, trembling imperceptibly, as if they were telling me, Don't be crazy, Auxilio, what are you thinking, go straight back to your rooftop room right now, forget Lilian and her infernal offspring, forget the Calle República de El Salvador, and forget this apartment which draws its sustenance from anti-life, from anti-matter, from the black holes of Mexico and Latin America, from all that once tried to find a way out into life but now leads only back to death.

And then I stopped looking at myself in the mirror and two or perhaps three tears welled from my eyes. Tears, how many nights have I spent pondering them, to come to such meager conclusions.

Then I went back to the living room and Coffeen was still there, standing, staring at a point in vacant space, and although when he heard me emerge from the passage (as one might emerge from a spaceship) he turned his head and looked at me, I knew immediately that he wasn't looking so much at me, his unexpected visitor, as at the life of the world outside, the life he had spurned, which, nevertheless, was eating him alive, even though he feigned a regal indifference. And then, more out of stubbornness than desire, I burned the last of my boats, sat down, uninvited, on the battered sofa, and repeated Lilian's words, telling him that she wouldn't be coming home that night, that he shouldn't worry, first thing next morning she'd be back, and I added a few words of my own, which weren't strictly relevant, banal remarks on the home of the poet and the painter, such a nice location, close to the center but in a calm, quiet street, and since I was there, I thought it wouldn't do any harm to inform him of the interest a number of people had expressed in his work; I said that I found his drawings, which his mother had shown me, interesting, an adjective that hardly seems adjectival at all, so varied are its functions, from describing a film that you don't want to admit you found boring to remarking on a woman's pregnancy. But *interesting* is also or can also be a synonym of mysterious. And I was talking about mystery. That was what I was really talking about. I think Coffeen understood, because after looking at me again with those exile's eyes of his, he took a chair (for a moment I thought he was going to hurl it at my head), and straddled it backward, gripping the bars of the backrest like a minimalist prisoner.

Then, as if I had heard the shot that signals the beginning of the hunting season, I remember I began to spout whatever came into my head. Until I ran out of words. Sometimes it seemed that Coffeen was about to fall asleep, and sometimes his knuckles clenched as if he was about to burst or as if the backrest of the chair that stood between him

and me was about to fly apart, explode, disinte-
grate. But there came a point, as I said, when I ran
out of words.

I don't think it was long before sunrise.

Then Coffeen spoke. He asked me if I knew the
story of Erigone. No, I don't, but the name's famil-
iar, I said (lying), afraid I was putting my foot in it.
For a moment, with a sinking heart, I thought he
was going to tell me about an ex-lover. We all have
an old love affair to talk about when there's noth-
ing left to say and day is breaking. But it turned out
that Erigone was not one of Coffeen's ex-lovers but
a figure from Greek mythology, the daughter of
Aegisthus and Clytemnestra. That's a story I do
know. A story I did know. Agamemnon goes off to
Troy and Clytemnestra becomes Aegisthus's mis-
tress. When Agamemnon comes back from Troy,
Aegisthus and Clytemnestra kill him, and then get
married. Electra and Orestes, the children of
Agamemnon and Clytemnestra, decide to avenge
their father and regain control of the kingdom.
This involves killing Aegisthus and their own
mother. Horror. I could get that far on my own. But
Coffeen Serpas went further. He spoke of the
daughter of Clytemnestra and Aegisthus, Erigone,
Orestes's half-sister, and said that she was the most
beautiful woman in all Greece; her mother's sister,

after all, was none other than Helen of Troy. He spoke of Orestes's vengeance. A spiritual hecatomb, he said. Do you know what a hecatomb is? I associated that word with nuclear warfare, so I thought it better not to reply. But Coffeen kept asking. A disaster, I said, a catastrophe? No, said Coffeen, a hecatomb is the sacrifice of a hundred oxen all at once. It comes from the Greek *hekaton*, which means one hundred, and *bous*, which means ox. There are even records from classical times of five hundred oxen being slain. Can you imagine that, he asked. Yes, I can imagine anything, I replied. The sacrifice of a hundred or five hundred oxen: you would have been able to smell the stench of blood for miles around. Imagine so much death, all around you; it must have been stupefying. Yes, I imagine it was, I said. Well, the vengeance of Orestes was something like that, said Coffeen. The terror and the irreparability of parricide, the shame and the panic, he said. And in the midst of that terror: Erigone, exquisite, immaculate, observing the intellectual Electra and the eponymous hero Orestes.

The intellectual Electra and the eponymous hero Orestes? For a moment I thought that Coffeen was pulling my leg.

But no, not at all. In fact Coffeen was talking as

if he were alone: with every word that came out of his mouth I was farther and farther away from that apartment on the Calle República de El Salvador. Although at the same time, however paradoxical it might seem, I was also more present, as an absence, as if the features of the immaculate Erigone were supplanting my invisible or reality-faded features, so that although, in a sense, I was disappearing, in another sense, as I disappeared my shadow took on the features of Erigone, and Erigone was present there, in the decrepit living room of Lilian's apartment, summoned by the words that Coffeen was reeling off, like a gossip or a busybody (as Julio Torri, who liked this sort of story, would have said), oblivious to my worried look, since although I was reluctant to leave him that night, I also realized that the path on which he had set out was perhaps the preamble to a nervous breakdown brought on by the absence of his mother, or by my unexpected presence, which was no compensation.

But Coffeen went on with his story.

And so I discovered that after the murder of Aegisthus, Orestes proclaimed himself king, and the followers of Aegisthus had to go into exile. Erigone, however, remained in the kingdom. The still Erigone, said Coffeen. Still under the vacant gaze of Orestes. Nothing but her extraordinary

ROBERTO BOLAÑO

beauty can momentarily placate his homicidal fury.
One night Orestes loses control, gets into her bed,
and rapes her.

He wakes up at first light the next day and goes
to the window: the lunar landscape of Argos con-
firms his suspicion. He has fallen in love with
Erigone. But someone who has killed his mother is
incapable of love, said Coffeen looking me in the
eye with a charred smile, and Orestes knows that
Erigone is poison to him, as well as being a blood
relative of Aegisthus, which is sufficient justifica-
tion for leading her to slaughter. Over the follow-
ing days, Orestes's followers persecute and elimi-
nate the followers of Aegisthus. At night, like a
drug addict or a wino (Coffeen's similes), Orestes
visits Erigone's bedchamber and they make love. In
the end, Erigone gets pregnant. Having found out,
Electra confronts her brother and explains why this
is an unsatisfactory state of affairs. Erigone, says
Electra, will give birth to a grandchild of Aegisthus.
There is no longer a single man in Argos who is a
blood relative of the usurper. Having taken it upon
himself to fell that tree, how can Orestes weaken
now and allow a new shoot to spring up? But it's
my child too, says Orestes. It's the grandchild of
Aegisthus, Electra insists. So Orestes accepts his sis-
ter's advice and decides to kill Erigone.

Nevertheless he wants to sleep with her one last time, so he does. She suspects nothing and gives herself to Orestes without fear. Although young, she has quickly learned how to handle the new king's madness. She calls him brother, my brother, she implores him, sometimes she pretends to see him and sometimes she pretends to see only a dark and solitary silhouette taking refuge in a corner of her bedchamber. (Was that Coffeen's idea of erotic ecstasy?) Before dawn, a besotted Orestes reveals his plan. He proposes an alternative. Erigone must leave Argos that very night. Orestes will provide a guide, who will take her out of the city and far away. Horrified, Erigone looks at him in the darkness (they are sitting at opposite ends of the bed), suspecting that Orestes's words conceal her death sentence: the guide that her brother says he is prepared to provide will turn out to be her executioner.

Seized by fear, she says that she would prefer to stay in the city, close to him.

Orestes loses his patience. If you stay here, I will kill you, he says. The gods have driven me crazy. Once again, he speaks of his crime; he speaks of the Erinnyes and the life he wants to lead when he can sort things out in his head or even before he gets them sorted out: wandering through Greece with his friend Pylades, becoming a legend. Hippies, with no ties to hold us, turning our lives into art. But Erigone doesn't understand Orestes's words, and fears that all this is part of a plan hatched by the cerebral Electra, a kind of euthanasia, an exit into darkness that will not stain the young king's hands with blood.

TWELVE

Orestes was moved by Erigone's misgivings, my friends. Or so Carlos Coffeen Serpas told me. He looked me in the eye and his whispered words emerged through a slit-like aperture, as if they were scalpel-sharp communion wafers. Then he said that it was only from that moment on, that is, *after* having been moved, that Orestes began to give serious thought to the idea of protecting Erigone from the dangers besetting her in devastated Argos, which consisted, fundamentally, of his own madness, his homicidal fury, his shame and repentance, that is, the components of what he liked to call the destiny of Orestes, a high-sounding name for self-destruction.

So Orestes spent the whole night talking with Erigone, and in the course of that night he bared his soul as never before; so numerous were his arguments and so skillfully expounded, that, shortly before dawn, Erigone finally yielded, accepting the guide that Orestes had offered. She left the city at first light.

From a tower, Orestes watched her walking away from the city. Then he shut his eyes and, when he opened them again, Erigone was nowhere to be seen.

As he said this, Coffeen shut his eyes, and I saw the moon (full, waning, or waxing—what did it matter?) racing at a vertiginous pace to touch every tile in the women's bathroom on the fourth floor of the Faculty of Philosophy and Literature in the unscathed year 1968. And I thought, as I had thought before, as I am thinking now, What shall I do? Make a run for it while his eyes are closed? Escape from that decrepit time-warp of an apartment? Or wait until he opens his eyes, and then ask him what that episode from Greek mythology meant, if anything? Sit quietly and close my own eyes, at the risk of opening them again to see not Coffeen and his dusty paintings but bathroom tiles illuminated by the moonlight that shimmered in that month of September on the campus of the UNAM? Realize that I had been playing with fire for long enough, snap out of it, say good night or good morning, and leave, turning my back on that apartment adrift in a Mexican wilderness of closed eyes? Or stretch out my hand, touch Coffeen's face, act as if I had understood his story (although I hadn't), and then go resolutely to the kitchen and brew some tea or, better still, two cups of lime blossom infusion.

I could have done any of those things. In the end, I did nothing.

Coffeen opened his eyes and looked at me. That's all, he said. He tried to smile, but he couldn't. Or maybe that grimace or nervous tic was his way of smiling. The rest of the story is pretty well known, he said. Orestes goes traveling with Pylades. At one point in his travels he meets his sister Iphigenia. He has adventures. He is renowned throughout Greece. At the mention of Iphigenia, I was about to say that Orestes would have done better to keep away from his poisonous sisters, but I didn't. And then Coffeen stood up, as if to make it clear to me that it was very late and that he wanted to get back to work or go to bed or consider the deeds of ancient Greeks on his own in a corner of the living room. The problem was that I had gone on thinking about Erigone and suddenly I realized something about the story that had escaped my notice until then. Something, something, but what?

Coffeen stood there frozen in a posture that was an invitation to leave, and I remained frozen on the sofa, while my gaze wandered over the floor, the furniture, the walls, even Coffeen's face. I was wearing the expression of someone who is about to remember something, or has a name on the tip of her tongue, a thought beginning to gestate among electrical impulses and currents of blood, but remaining in the shadows, as it were, formless, frightened of itself or of the mechanism it has set in motion, or rather frightened of the effect that it will inevitably have on that mechanism, and yet unable to delay the connection or the revelation, as if by dint of repetition the name Erigone had become a kind of forceps dragging whatever it was from its lair, to an accompaniment of howls, involuntary giggles and sundry atrocities.

And then, before I knew what it was that I had remembered or thought, Coffeen said that it was very late, and walked nervously across that room encumbered with the objects that in former times had constituted the comfort and luxury of Lilian Serpas's home, avoiding them with an agility which can only be acquired through habit.

Cronus, I said. I was thinking of the story of Cronus. Do you know it? I asked in a shrill tone of voice, not so much a relic of my Rio de la Plata accent as a self-defense mechanism. The story of Cronus, of course I do, said Coffeen, his eyes filmed with some kind of solvent. I don't know why I thought of it, I said, stalling for time. It doesn't have anything to do with Orestes, said Coffeen. Aha, I replied, without covering my mouth, looking at one of Coffeen's drawings on the wall, hoping it would help me find something to say. The drawing showed a man walking along a path, watched by stars that had eyes. To be frank, it was abysmal. To be frank, it was no spur to eloquence at all. To be frank, I was at a lost for words, and for a moment—as if for the span of a lightning flash I had seen through appearances to the other side—it seemed that Coffeen was Orestes and I was Erigone, which meant that the night would have no end, I would never see the light of day again, I would be incinerated by the black gaze of Lilian's son, and as my speculations ran wild and my fear mounted steadily (although without spreading), assuming the proportions of a birch or an oak, a vast tree in the midst of a vast night, the only tree on a lonely plain, Coffeen opened his eyes, eyes that had seen Erigone disappear in the vastness of time, and looked at me with a gaze that was blank for a moment or perplexed, the sort of gaze that settles on a perfect stranger or a random configuration of shapes, but as he gradually recognized me, perplexity gave way to hatred, rancor, and homicidal fury.

And then I understood and seized upon what had escaped my notice until then.

Hold on, I said. Now I remember, I said. The air had been thick with thousands of flying insects, but now it cleared. Coffeen was looking at me. I was looking at an airport devoid of planes and people, from whose shadowless hangars and runways only dreams and visions departed. It was the airport of the drunks and the drug addicts. But then it evaporated and in its place I saw Coffeen's eyes wanting to know what it was that I had remembered. And I said: Nothing. Nothing, just some crazy idea I had. I went to get up, because by then I really did feel it was time to go, but Coffeen put his hand on my shoulder and stopped me. Let God's will be done, I thought. I am not a religious woman, but that was what ran through my mind. And: I shall not see the light of a new day, which,

put like that, sounds rather trite, but for me, at that
moment, those words had the ring of a mysterious
portal, or something. And, strange as it may seem,
what I felt was not fear but relief, as if I had been
anesthetized by suddenly realizing what I had over-
looked in the story of Erigone, and although there
was nothing clinical, to say the least, about the liv-
ing room of Lilian Serpas's apartment, I felt as
though I was being wheeled into an operating
room. I thought: I am in the women's bathroom in
the Faculty of Philosophy and Literature and I am
the last person left. I was heading for the operating
room. I was heading for the birth of History. And
since I'm not a complete idiot, I also thought: It's
over now, the riot police have left the university, the
students have died at Tlatelolco, the university has
opened again, but I'm still shut up in the fourth-
floor bathroom, as if after all my scratching at the
moonlit tiles a door had opened, but not the portal
of sadness in the continuum of Time. They have all
gone, except me. They have all come back, except
me. The second affirmation was hard to accept,
because in fact I couldn't see anyone, and if they
had all come back I would have been able to see
them. In fact, all I could see, strain as I might, were
the eyes of Carlos Coffeen Serpas. Still the vague
certitude remained, as my trolley was wheeled down

the corridor, a forest-green corridor with stretches
of camouflage and bottle green, toward an operat-
ing room dilating in time, as History announced its
birth with raucous cries and the doctors diagnosed
my anemia in whispers, but how are they going to
operate for anemia, I wondered. I barely managed
to whisper, Am I going to have a baby, doctor? The
doctors looked down at me, wearing their green
bank-robber's masks, and said, No, as the trolley
accelerated on its way down a corridor that was
writhing like a loose vein. I'm not going to have a
baby, really? I'm not pregnant? I asked. And the
doctors looked at me and said, No, Ma'am, we're
just taking you to attend the birth of History. But
what's the hurry, doctor? I feel dizzy! And the doc-
tors replied with the patter they use on the dying:
The birth of History can't wait, and if we arrive late
you won't see anything, only ruins and smoke, an
empty landscape, and you'll be alone again forever
even if you go out and get drunk with your poet
friends every night. Well, let's get a move on, then,
I said. The anesthesia was going to my head, over-
whelming me as homesickness sometimes does,
and I stopped asking questions (for a while). I fixed
my gaze on the ceiling and all I could hear were the
rubber wheels of the trolley trundling along and
the muted cries of other patients, other victims of

Pentothal (that's what I thought), and I even felt a pleasant, gentle warmth creeping up my long, frozen bones.

When we reached the operating room, the vision misted over, cracked, fell and shattered, and then the fragments were pulverized by a bolt of lightning, and a gust of wind blew the dust away to nowhere or spread it through Mexico City.

It was time to open my eyes again and say something, anything, to Carlos Coffeen Serpas.

So I said it was late and that I should go. And Coffeen looked at me as if he too had seen something that can normally be seen only in dreams. He stepped back abruptly. Your mother will be home again tomorrow morning, I said. All right, said Coffeen, looking away.

He accompanied me to the door. As I was going down the first flight of stairs, I turned around; he was still there on the landing, watching me, with the door open. I lifted my hand to my mouth and started to say something but soon realized that I was pronouncing incoherent syllables. It was as if I had suddenly become demented. So I stood there with my hand over my mouth, looking at him, unable to speak, until Coffeen closed the door with an expression compounded, as far as I could tell, of fear and fatigue in equal parts. For a few seconds I remained there motionless. I was thinking. Then the light in the stairwell went out and I started going slowly down the stairs, in the darkness, holding on to the banister.

I hailed a taxi on Bolívar.

As it was taking me to my rooftop room, which at the time was in Colonia Escandón, I started crying. The driver glanced across at me. He looked like an iguana. I think he thought I was a whore going home after a hard night. Don't cry, blondie, he said, it's not worth it, things'll look different tomorrow, you'll see. Instead of philosophizing, I said, Why don't you watch where you're going.

By the time I got out of the cab, I had stopped crying.

I made myself a cup of tea, got into bed, and tried to read. I can't remember what. Certainly not Pedro Garfías. Eventually I gave up and drank my tea with the light off. Then day broke once again over the capital of Mexico.

Then I realized what was going on and a fragile, tremulous joy came into my days. My nights with the poets of Mexico City left me exhausted, empty, or on the verge of tears. I moved to a new rooftop room. I lived in Colonia Napoles and Colonia Roma and Colonia Atenor Salas. I lost my books and I lost my clothes. But soon I came by other books and, eventually, other clothes as well. I picked up odd jobs at the university and lost them again. I was there every day, circumstances permitting, and saw things that no one else was there to see. My beloved Faculty of Philosophy and Literature, with its Florentine feuds and Roman vendettas. From time to time I ran into Lilian Serpas at the Café Quito or some other place on the Avenida Bucareli and, naturally, we said hello, but we never mentioned her beloved son (although some nights I would have given anything to be asked to go to her apartment again and tell him that she wouldn't be coming home), until at some point she stopped turning up in my haunts like a ghost in a storm, and no one asked after her, and I didn't feel like inquiring about her whereabouts, my spirit had become so fragile, I was so devoid of the curiosity that, in former times, had been one of my most salient traits.

Not long afterward I started sleeping a lot. I never used to sleep much before that. I was the insomniac of Mexican poetry; I read all the poems and praised them all and never missed a gathering. But one day, a few months after having seen Carlos Coffeen Serpas for the first and last time, I fell asleep on a bus to the university and only woke up when someone took me by the shoulders and shook me as if they were trying to get a broken clock going. I woke with a start. It was a boy of about seventeen who had woken me, a student, and when I saw his face I could barely hold back my tears.

From that day on, sleeping became a vice.

I didn't want to think about Coffeen or the story of Erigone and Orestes. I didn't want to think about my own story and the years I had left to live.

So I slept, wherever I happened to be, mainly when I was alone (it was an escape from solitude—as soon as I was on my own, I'd fall asleep), but as time went by the vice became chronic, and I started falling asleep in public, leaning on a table in some bar or sitting on a hard seat at some student play.

At night the guardian angel of my dreams would come to me and say: Hey, Auxilio, so now you know where they ended up, the kids of Latin America. Shut up, I replied. Shut up. I don't know anything. What do you mean, the kids? I don't know anything at all. Then the voice made a murmuring sound; it said, Mmm, or something like that, as if it found my answer unconvincing. And I said: I'm still in the women's bathroom in the Faculty of Philosophy and Literature, and the moon is melting the tiles on the wall one by one, opening a hole for images to flow through, films about us and the books we read, and the future moving at the speed of light, which we shall not see.

And then I dreamed of idiotic prophecies.

And the small voice said, Hey, Auxilio, what can you see?

The future, I replied. I can see what the future holds for the books of the twentieth century.

And can you make any prophecies, asked the voice, sounding curious, but not in the least ironic.

I don't know about prophecies as such, but I can make a prediction or two, I replied with a dreamer's syrupy voice.

Go on, go on, said the small voice, with unbridled enthusiasm.

I am in the women's bathroom in the faculty building and I can see the future, I said, in a soprano voice, as if I were being coy.

I know that, said the dream voice, I know that. You start making your prophecies and I'll note them down.

Voices, I said in a baritone voice, don't note things down, they don't even listen. Voices only speak.

You're wrong about that, but it doesn't matter, you say what you have to say, and try to say it loud and clear.

Then I took a deep breath, hesitated, let my mind go blank and finally said: These are my prophecies.

Vladimir Mayakovksy shall come back into fashion around the year 2150. James Joyce shall be reincarnated as a Chinese boy in the year 2124. Thomas Mann shall become a Ecuadorian pharmacist in the year 2101.

For Marcel Proust, a desperate and prolonged period of oblivion shall begin in the year 2033. Ezra Pound shall disappear from certain libraries in the year 2089. Vachel Lindsay shall appeal to the masses in the year 2101.

César Vallejo shall be read underground in the year 2045. Jorge Luis Borges shall be read underground in the year 2045. Vicente Huidobro shall appeal to the masses in the year 2101.

Virginia Woolf shall be reincarnated as an Argentinean fiction writer in the year 2076. Louis-Ferdinand Céline shall enter Purgatory in the year 2094. Paul Eluard shall appeal to the masses in the year 2101.

Metempsychosis. Poetry shall not disappear. Its non-power shall manifest itself in a different form.

Cesare Pavese shall become the patron saint of Seers and Lookers in the year 2034. Pier Paolo Pasolini shall become the patron saint of Escapees in the year 2100. Giorgio Bassani shall emerge from his tomb in the year 2167.

Oliverio Girondo shall come into his own as a children's writer in the year 2099. The complete works of Roberto Arlt shall be adapted for the

ROBERTO BOLAÑO

screen in 2102. The complete works of Adolfo Bioy
Casares shall be adapted for the screen in 2105.

Arno Schmidt shall rise from his ashes in the
year 2085. Franz Kafka shall once again be read
underground throughout Latin America in the year
2101. Witold Gombrowicz shall enjoy great pres-
tige in the environs of the Río de la Plata around
the year 2098.

Paul Celan shall rise from his ashes in the year
2113. André Breton shall return through mirrors in
the year 2071. Max Jacob shall cease to be read,
that is to say his last reader shall die, in the year
2059.

Who shall read Jean-Pierre Duprey in the year
2059? Who shall read Gary Snyder? Who shall
read Ilarie Voronca? These are the questions I ask
myself.

Who shall read Gilberte Dallas? Who shall read
Rodolfo Wilcock? Who shall read Alexandre Unik?

A statue of Nicanor Parra, however, shall stand
in a Chilean square in the year 2059. A statue of
Octavio Paz shall stand in a Mexican square in
the year 2020. A rather small statue of Ernesto
Cardenal shall stand in a Nicaraguan square in the
year 2018.

But all statues tumble eventually, by divine
intervention or the power of dynamite, like the

statue of Heine. So let us not place too much trust in statues.

Carson McCullers, however, shall go on being read in the year 2100. Alejandra Pizarnik shall lose her last reader in the year 2100. Alfonsina Storni shall be reincarnated as a cat or a sea-lion, I can't tell which, in the year 2050.

The case of Anton Chekhov shall be slightly different: he shall be reincarnated in the year 2003, in the year 2010, and then in the year 2014. He shall appear once more in the year 2081. And never again after that.

Alice Sheldon shall appeal to the masses in the year 2017. Alfonso Reyes shall be killed once and for all in the year 2058, but in fact it shall be Reyes who kills his killers. Marguerite Duras shall live in the nervous system of thousands of women in the year 2035.

And the little voice said, How strange, how strange, I haven't read some of those authors you mentioned.

Which ones? I asked.

Well, that Alice Sheldon, for example. I have no idea who she is.

I laughed. I laughed for quite a while. What's so funny, asked the little voice. Having caught you out, you being so cultured and all, I answered.

Cultured, I don't know if I'm cultured, whatever that means, but I have read a bit. How odd, I said, as if the dream had suddenly swung 180 degrees and I was now in some cold place, populated by multiple Popocatepetls and Ixtacihuatls. What's odd, asked the little voice. The fact that the angel of my dreams is from Buenos Aires when I'm Uruguyuan. Ah, well, that's quite common, actually, she said. Alice Sheldon publishes her books under the pseudonym James Tiptree Jr., I said, shivering from the cold. I haven't read them, said the voice. She writes science fiction, stories and novels, I said. I haven't read them. I haven't read them, said the voice, and I could distinctly hear the sound of chattering teeth. Do you have teeth? I asked incredulously.

Not real, genuine teeth of my own, no, she replied. But when I'm with you, all your missing teeth chatter for me. My teeth! I thought with some affection but not a trace of nostalgia. This cold is unbearable, don't you think, said my guardian angel. Yes, it's very, very cold, I said. What do you say we get out of this ice-box, the voice proposed. That's a great idea, I said, but I don't know how we'll manage that. You'd have to be a mountain climber to get out of here without smashing your skull.

For a while we moved across the ice, trying to make out Mexico City in the distance.

This reminds me of a picture by Caspar David Friedrich, said the little voice. I knew you'd say that, I replied. What do you mean by that, she asked. Nothing, nothing.

And then, hours or months later, the little voice said, We're going to have to walk out of here, no one is going to come and rescue us. And I said to her, We can't, we'll smash our skulls (or I will). Anyway, I'm starting to get used to the cold and the purity of this air; it's as if we had gone back to live in Dr. Atl's most transparent region, with a vengeance. And the little voice looked at me with a sound as sad and crystalline as Rimbaud's poem about the vowels and said, You've become used to it.

And then, some months or maybe years of silence later, she said to me, You remember those compatriots of yours who had a plane accident? Which compatriots? I asked, tired of that voice interrupting my dreams of nothing. The ones who crashed in the Andes and everyone had given up hope and they were up in the mountains for something like three months, eating the dead bodies so as not to die of hunger, I think they were soccer players, said the little voice. They were rugby players, I said. Rugby players? That's funny, I thought

ROBERTO BOLAÑO

they were soccer players. Anyway, so you remember them? Yes, I remember them, the rugby-playing cannibals of the Andes. Well, that's what you should do, said the little voice.

Who am I supposed to eat? I said, looking for her shadow, which sounded as sweet and emphatic as Ruben Darío's "Marcha Triunfal." Not me, you can't eat me, said the little voice. Who can I eat then? I'm alone here. There's you and me and the thousands of Popocatepetls and Ixtaccihuatls and the icy wind and nothing else, I said as I walked through the snow and scanned the horizon for any sign of Latin America's biggest city. But Mexico fucking City was nowhere to be seen and what I really wanted to do was to go back to sleep.

Then the little voice began to talk about the end of a novel by Julio Cortázar, the one where a character is dreaming that he's in a movie theater and someone comes along and tells him to wake up. And she started talking about Marcel Schwob and Jerzy Andrzejewski and Pitol's translation of Andrzejewski's novel, and I said, Hold it, will you, I know all that already, my problem, if it really is a problem, isn't how to wake up but how to fall asleep again, which is pretty strange, since I have pleasant dreams and no one wants to wake up from a pleasant dream. To which the little voice replied in psychoanalytic jargon, which dispelled any doubts I might have had about her city of origin: definitely Buenos Aires, not Montevideo. Then I said to her, That's funny, my shivers are usually Uruguayan, but the guardian angel of my dreams is Argentinean. To which she replied, in a professorial tone, Indeed she is.

And then we remained silent, while the wind fitfully whipped up necklaces of ice that hung in the air for a few seconds before disappearing; both of us were scanning the featureless horizon so as not to miss the silhouette of Mexico City should it appear somewhere, although, to tell the truth, we held out little hope.

Finally the little voice said, Hey, Auxilio, I better get going. Where to, I asked her. To another dream, she said. Which dream, I asked. Any other dream, she said, I'm freezing to death here. And she said this with such heart-felt sincerity that I looked for her face in the snow and when at last I found her little face it sounded just like a poem by Robert Frost about the snow and the cold, and that made me very sad, because the little voice was not lying— it was true that she was freezing, poor thing.

So I took her in my arms to warm her up and said to her, You go whenever you like, that's absolutely fine. I would have liked to say something more, but those rather uninspired words were all I could muster. And the little voice moved in my arms like the fluff on a weightless angora sweater, and purred like the cats in Remedios Varo's garden. And when she had warmed up I told her, Go on, it's been a pleasure to meet you, go before you start to freeze again. The little voice slipped out of my arms (but it was as if she had come out of my navel) and off she went without saying Goodbye or Ciao or anything, she took French leave, like a good Argentinean guardian angel, and I was left alone, with my thoughts running wild, and the upshot of all that cogitation was, in the end, that the little voice had made me spout utter nonsense. You've made a fool of yourself, I said aloud, or at least I tried to say it aloud.

I say I tried because that was all I could do: open my mouth and attempt to form those words in the snowbound wilderness, but the cold was so intense that I couldn't even move my jaws. So I suppose I only thought what I was trying to say, although I should add that my thoughts were deafening (or so they seemed to me among those snowy heights), as if the cold, while numbing and killing me, were simultaneously turning me into a kind of yeti, a muscle-bound snow-woman, hirsute and stentorian, although of course I knew that this was all in my imagination, I hadn't acquired bulging muscles or long hair to protect me from the icy blasts or, least of all, a voice resonant as a cathedral, a self-sufficient voice with no function but to articulate a single, vacuous, hollow, insomniac's question—Why? Why?—until the walls of ice began to split and come crashing down with a huge din, while others reared up behind the screen of dust raised by the collapse, so that there was nothing to be done; it was inexorable, hopeless, futile, everything, even crying, because on the snowy heights, as I was astonished to learn, people do not cry, they only ask questions; on the heights of Machu Picchu no one cries, either because their tear ducts have frozen up or because at that altitude even tears are futile, which, however you look at it, is the limit.

So there I was, cradled in snow and prepared to die, when suddenly I heard something dripping and I said to myself, How can that be? I must be hallucinating again, nothing drips in the high Himalayas, everything is frozen solid. That little sound was enough to stop me falling into an everlasting sleep. I opened my eyes and tried to see where it was coming from. I thought, Could the glacier be melting? The darkness seemed almost absolute, but it was just that my eyes were taking some time to adjust, as I soon discovered. Then I saw the still moon reflected in a tile, a single tile, as if it was waiting for me. I was sitting on the floor, resting my back against the wall. I got up. The faucet in one of the sinks in the women's bathroom on the fourth floor was not properly turned off. I turned it on and splashed my face. Then the moon changed tiles.

That was when I decided to come down from the mountains. I decided not to starve to death in the women's bathroom. I decided not to go crazy. I decided not to become a beggar. I decided to tell the truth even if it meant being pointed at. I began my descent. All I can remember is the freezing wind like a blade against my face and the moon glowing. There were rocks and ravines; there were post-nuclear ski slopes. But I didn't let them bother me; I continued my descent. Somewhere in the sky an electric storm was brewing, but I didn't worry too much about that. I was thinking happy thoughts as I continued my descent. I was thinking about Arturito Belano, for example, and how, when he came back to Mexico City, he started hanging out with new friends, kids who were younger than him and the other young poets of Mexico: sixteen, seventeen, eighteen years old. And then he met Ulises Lima and began to laugh at his old friends, including me, forgiving their errant ways, as if he were Dante and had just returned from Hell, what am I saying, as if he were Virgil himself, such a sensitive boy, he started smoking marijuana, commonly known as weed, and messing with substances I would rather not even imagine. But for all that, deep down, he was, I knew, the same sweet kid he had always been. And so, when we happened to meet, by sheer chance because we weren't hanging out with the same crowd anymore, he would say, How's it going, Auxilio, or play on my name, calling out Help, Help! Help!! from the opposite sidewalk on the Avenida Bucareli, leaping around like a monkey with a taco or a slice of pizza in his hand; he was always with Laura Jáuregi, his girlfriend, who was very pretty, but also supremely arrogant, and Ulises Lima and that other young Chilean, Felipe Müller, and sometimes I even plucked up my courage and joined them, but they spoke Gliglish, and although it was clear that they liked me and knew who I was, they talked Gliglish amongst themselves, which made it hard for me to understand the ins and outs of the conversation, so in the end I went back to following my path through the snow.

But don't think they were making fun of me! They listened to what I said. But I didn't speak Gliglish and they simply couldn't stop using their private slang, poor kids. Poor forsaken kids. Because that's what they were: no one loved them. Or no one took them seriously. Or only they did; too much, I sometimes felt.

And one day someone told me that Arturito Belano had left Mexico. Then added: This time, let's hope he doesn't come back. And that made me furious, because I had always liked Arturito and I think I probably insulted that person (mentally, at least), but first I had the presence of mind to ask where Arturito had gone. The person didn't know: Australia, Europe, Canada, somewhere like that. Afterward I kept thinking about him, and about his mother, who was so generous, and his sister, and the afternoons we spent together at their apartment making empanadas, and the time I made noodles and we hung them up to dry all over the place, in the kitchen, the dining room and the little living room they had in that apartment on the Calle Abraham González.

I can't forget anything. That's my problem, or so I've been told.

I am the mother of Mexico's poets. I am the only one who held out in the university in 1968, when the riot police and the army came in. I stayed there on my own in the Faculty, shut up in a bathroom, with no food, for more than ten days, for more than fifteen days, from the eighteenth to the thirtieth of September, I think, I'm not sure any more.

I stayed there with a book by Pedro Garfías and my satchel, wearing a little white blouse and a pleated sky-blue skirt, and I had more than enough time to think things over. But I couldn't think about Arturo Belano, because I hadn't met him yet.

I said to myself: Hang in there, Auxilio Lacouture. If you go out they'll arrest you (and probably deport you to Montevideo, because, naturally, your immigration papers aren't in order, you silly girl), they'll spit on you and beat you up. I prepared myself to endure. To endure hunger and solitude. For the first few hours I slept sitting in the stall, the one I was in when it all began, because in my destitution I believed that it would bring me luck, but sleeping on a throne is extremely uncomfortable, and in the end I curled up on the tiles. I had dreams, not nightmares but musical dreams, dreams about transparent questions, dreams of slender, safe airplanes flying the length and breadth of Latin America through skies of brilliant, cold blue. I woke up frozen stiff and ravenous. I looked out of the window, the little round window over the sinks, and saw the new day dawning in pieces of the campus like pieces of a puzzle. I spent that first morning crying and thanking the angels in Heaven that they hadn't cut off the water. Don't get sick, Auxilio, I told myself, drink all the water you like, but don't get sick. I leaned against the wall and let myself slide to the ground, and once again I opened that book by Pedro Garfías. My eyes closed. I must have fallen asleep. Then I heard steps and hid in my stall (it was the nun's cell I never had, my trench and my Duino Palace, my Mexican epiphany). I read Pedro Garfías. Then I fell asleep. Then I looked out of the bull's-eye window and saw very high clouds and thought of Dr. Atl's pictures and the most transparent region. Then I started thinking pleasant thoughts.

How many lines of poetry did I know by heart? I started reciting, murmuring the lines I could remember, and I would have liked to write them down, but although I had a ball-point pen, I didn't have any paper. Then I thought: Silly, you have all the paper you need. So I ripped off squares of toilet paper and began to write. Then I fell asleep and dreamed, and this is really funny, I dreamed of Juana de Ibarbourou and her book *La rosa de los vientos* (The Compass Rose), published in 1930, and her first book too, *Las lenguas de diamante* (Diamond Tongues), such a pretty title, exquisite, it could be the title of an avant-garde book published last year in French, but Juana de America published it in 1919, at the age of twenty-seven. What a fascinating woman she must have been then, with the world at her feet and all those gentlemen gallantly prepared to do her bidding (they are all gone now, although Juana remains), all those modernist poets prepared to give their lives for poetry, so many glances and compliments, so much love.

Then I woke up. I thought: I am the memory.

That's what I thought. Then I went back to sleep. Then I woke up, and for hours, maybe days, I cried for times gone by, for my childhood in Montevideo, for faces that disturb me (even now, more than ever, in fact), faces of which I prefer not to speak.

Then I lost count of the days I'd spent shut up in there. From my little window I saw birds, segments of tree trunks or branches growing from somewhere invisible, shrubs, grass, clouds, walls, but I couldn't see people or hear noises, and I lost track of the time I had been shut up in there. Then, maybe remembering Charlie Chaplin, I ate toilet paper, but only a little, I couldn't stomach more. Then I realized that I was no longer hungry. Then I picked up all the pieces of toilet paper on which I had written, threw them in the toilet and pulled the chain. The sound of the water gave me a start, and I thought I was finished.

I thought, In spite of all my cunning and self-sacrifice, I'm finished. I thought, How poetic, to destroy my writings like that. I thought, It would have been better to swallow them, now I'm finished. I thought, The vanity of writing, the vanity of destruction. I thought, Because I wrote, I endured. I thought, Because I destroyed what I had written, they will find me, they will hit me, they will rape me, they will kill me. I thought, The two things are connected, writing and destroying, hiding and being found. Then I sat down on the throne and shut my eyes. I fell asleep. Then I woke up again.

My whole body was stiff. I moved slowly across the bathroom, looked at myself in the mirror, combed my hair, washed my face. My face looked terrible! Like it does now, to give you some idea.

Then I heard voices. I don't think I'd heard any sound at all for a long time. I felt like Robinson Crusoe when he finds the footprint in the sand. But my footprint was a voice and a door slamming, my footprint was an avalanche of pebbles or marbles suddenly hurtling down the corridor. Then Lupita, Professor Fombona's secretary, opened the door and we stood there staring at each other, gaping, speechless. I think it was the emotional shock that made me pass out.

When I opened my eyes again, I was in Professor Rius's office (what a brave, handsome man he was, and is), among friends and familiar faces, university people, not soldiers, which was so wonderful that I began to cry, and couldn't tell my story coherently, although the professor kept enjoining me to do so, appalled by what I had endured, but equally grateful for it, I think.

And that is all, my friends. The legend was borne on the winds of Mexico City, the winds of 1968; it went among the dead and the survivors, and now everyone knows that when the university was occupied in that beautiful, ill-fated year, a woman remained on the campus. I went on living (although something—what I had seen—was missing), and often I would hear my story told by others, who said that the woman who had gone without food for thirteen days, shut up in the bath-room, was a medical student, or a secretary from the administration building, not an illegal alien from Uruguay, with no job and no place of her own to lay her head. Sometimes it wasn't even a woman but a man, a Maoist student or a professor with gastrointestinal problems. And when I heard those stories, those versions of my story, usually (if I was-n't drunk) I held my peace. And if I was drunk, I played the whole thing down. What does it matter, I would say, that's just university folklore, another of Mexico's City's urban legends, and they would look at me (but who were they?) and say: Auxilio, you're the mother of Mexican poetry. And I would say (or shout, if I was drunk), No, I'm nobody's mother, but I did know them all, all the young poets, whether they were natives of Mexico City, or came from the provinces, or other parts of Latin America and washed up here, and I loved them all.

Then they would look at me in silence.

And I would allow a judicious period to elapse before letting my gaze return to them, pretending not to understand and wondering why they weren't saying anything. And although I tried to look else-where, at the traffic passing in the street, the leisurely movement of the waitresses, or the smoke emerging from somewhere behind the bar, it was them I really wanted to watch, sitting there steeped in an endless silence, and it struck me as unnatural that they should be quiet for so long.

And at that point the anxiety returned, along with the wild speculation, the sleepiness, and the cold that lacerates your extremities before numbing them. But I didn't stop moving. I moved my arms and legs. I breathed. I oxygenated my blood. If I don't want to die, I'm not going to die, I told myself. So I moved, and at the same time, although there were no eagles to be seen, I had an eagle's eye view of my body moving through snowy passes, drifts and endless white esplanades like the back of a fossilized Moby Dick. Still I kept walking. I walked and walked. And from time to time I stopped and said to myself: Wake up, Auxilio. Nobody can endure this. And yet I knew I could endure it. So I baptized my right leg Willpower and my left leg Necessity. And I endured.

I endured, and one afternoon I left the immense regions of snow behind and saw a valley before me. I sat down and surveyed it. It was vast. It was like the background of some Renaissance painting, blown up enormously. The air was cold on my face, but not biting. I stopped on the slope above the valley and sat down. I was tired. I wanted to catch my breath. I didn't know what would become of me. Maybe, I speculated, someone would find me a job at the university. I breathed. The air tasted good. The light was fading. The sun was setting far away, over other valleys, each one unique, and smaller perhaps than the vast valley I had discovered. There was still a reasonable ambient brightness. As soon as I've regained some strength, I'll begin the descent, I thought, and before night falls I'll be in the valley.

I stood up. My legs trembled. I sat down again. There was a patch of snow a few yards from where I was. I went over to it and washed my face. I sat down again. A little farther down the slope was a tree. I saw a sparrow on one of its branches. Then there was a green streak in the air. I saw a quetzal. I saw a sparrow and a quetzal. The two birds perched on the same branch. My parted lips whispered, The same branch. I heard my voice. Only then was I aware of the enormous silence hanging over the valley.

I stood up and approached the tree. Carefully, because I didn't want to frighten the birds. From there, the view was better. But I had to walk gingerly, looking down, because there were loose stones and the chances of slipping and falling were high. When I reached the tree, the birds had flown away. Then I saw that at its far end, to the west, the valley opened into a bottomless abyss.

Am I going crazy? I wondered. Is this the madness and the fear of Arthur Gordon Pym? Or am I recovering my sanity so quickly it's making me dizzy? The words exploded in my head, as if a giant were shouting inside me, but outside the silence was total. To the west, the sun was setting; the shadows down in the valley were lengthening. What had been green before was now dark green, and what had been brown was dark gray or black.

Then, at the eastern end of the valley, I saw a different shadow, like that of a cloud sweeping across a broad field, but no cloud was throwing this shadow. What is it? I wondered. I looked at the sky. Then I looked at the tree and saw that the quetzal and the sparrow had returned and, sitting still on the same branch, were enjoying the quietness of the valley. Then I looked at the abyss. My heart clenched. The valley led straight into the abyss. I couldn't remember having seen a landform like that before. In fact, at that moment, I felt as if I were on a plateau rather than in a valley. But no. It wasn't a plateau. Plateaus, by their very nature, are not enclosed by natural walls. Valleys, on the other hand, I thought, do not plunge into bottomless abysses. Although perhaps some do. Then I looked at the shadow that was spreading and advancing

from the other end of the valley, as if it too had
emerged from the snowbound region, although at
a different point from myself. In the distance, over
the multiplied volcanoes, a thunderstorm was qui-
etly brewing. Then I realized that the quetzal and
the sparrow on the branch five feet above me were
the only living birds in that entire valley. And I real-
ized that the shadow sweeping the broad field was
a multitude of young people, an interminable
legion of young people on the march to some-
where.

I saw them. I was too far away to see their faces.
But I saw them. I don't know if they were creatures
of flesh and blood or ghosts. But I saw them.

They were probably ghosts.

But they were walking, not flying as they say
ghosts do. So perhaps they weren't ghosts. I also
realized that although they were walking together
they did not constitute what is commonly known
as a mass: their destinies were not oriented by a
common idea. They were united only by their gen-
erosity and courage. With the palms of my hands
pressed against my cheeks, I conjectured that they
too had wandered through the snowy mountains,
where they had met with one another and gradually
gathered to form the army that was now moving
across the field. They were on one side and I was on

the other. Flouting the laws of physics, the mountain peaks seemed to form a kind of mirror, with two sides: I had come out one side and they had come out the other.

They were walking toward the abyss. I think I realized that as soon as I saw them. A shadow or a mass of children, walking unstoppably toward the abyss.

Then I heard a murmur that rose through the cold air of evening in the valley toward the mountainsides and crags, and I was astonished.

They were singing.

The children, the young people, were singing and heading for the abyss. I raised a hand to my mouth, as if to stifle a shout, and held the other hand out in front of me, fingers extended and trembling, as if trying to touch them. My mind endeavored to remember a text about children intoning canticles as they marched to war. But it was no use. My mind was inside out. The journey through the snow had turned me into skin. Perhaps that is how I had always been. Intelligence has never been my strength.

I held out both hands, as if imploring the sky to let me embrace them, and I shouted, but my shout was lost among the heights and did not reach down into the valley. Thin, wrinkled, gravely wounded, my mind bleeding and my eyes full of tears, I looked for the birds as if those poor creatures could be of any help to me when the whole world was facing extinction.

They were not on the branch.

I presumed that the birds were a symbol or an emblem and that everything in that part of the story was simple and straightforward. I presumed that the birds stood for the children. I don't know what else I presumed.

And I heard them sing. I hear them singing still, faintly, even now that I am no longer in the valley, a barely audible murmur, the prettiest children of Latin America, the ill-fed and the well-fed children, those who had everything and those who had nothing, such a beautiful song it is, issuing from their lips, and how beautiful they were, such beauty, although they were marching deathward, shoulder to shoulder. I heard them sing and I went mad; I heard them sing and there was nothing I could do to make them stop, I was too far away and I didn't have the strength to go down into the valley, to stand in the middle of that field and tell them to stop, tell them they were marching toward certain death. The only thing I could do was to stand up, trembling, and listen to their song, go on listening to their song right up to the last breath, because, although they were swallowed by the abyss, the song remained in the air of the valley, in the mist of the valley rising toward the mountain-sides and the crags as evening drew on.

So the ghost-children marched down the valley and fell into the abyss. Their passage was brief. And their ghost-song or its echo, which is almost to say the echo of nothingness, went on marching, I could hear it marching on at the same pace, the pace of courage and generosity. A barely audible song, a song of war and love, because although the children were clearly marching to war, the way they marched recalled the superb, theatrical attitudes of love.

But what kind of love could they have known, I wondered when they were gone from the valley, leaving only their song resonating in my ears. The love of their parents, the love of their dogs and cats, the love of their toys, but above all the love, the desire and the pleasure they shared with one another.

And although the song that I heard was about war, about the heroic deeds of a whole generation of young Latin Americans led to sacrifice, I knew that above and beyond all, it was about courage and mirrors, desire and pleasure.

And that song is our amulet.